WITHOUT REMORSE

BLAIR HOWARD

ALSO BY BLAIR HOWARD

The Harry Starke Novels

Harry Starke

Two for the Money

Hill House

Checkmate

Gone

Family Matters

Retribution

Calypso

Without Remorse

Calaway Jones

Emoji

Hoodwinked

Apocalypse

The Lt. Kate Gazzara Novels

Jasmine

Saffron

Sapphire

Civil War Series

Chickamauga

ISBN-13: 978-1542303422

Published in the United States of America

 Created with Vellum

WITHOUT REMORSE

A Harry Starke Novel

By

Blair Howard

DEDICATED TO:

For Jo
Of Course

1

FRIDAY, MAY 3, 2002

It had been unseasonably warm in that part of Tennessee for weeks, and Friday was no exception. Peter Nicholson was sweating as he pushed his way through the dense undergrowth, out onto the narrow woodland path in the heart of Prentice Cooper State Forest. It was late afternoon, just after four; it had been a long day and he was tired. He'd bagged his limit: just one bird. He never had been able to figure that one out. Wild turkeys were more than plentiful in Prentice Cooper.

He propped his gun against the stump of an old iron-wood tree, held the bird up by its feet, shoved his glasses up the bridge of his nose, and inspected his prize. It was a fully adult hen, fat and healthy.

Not bad, he thought. *Maybe eight and a half... nine pounds. Great shot.* He smiled as he looked at the head-less carcass. *Clean as a whistle. Took it off like a bloody guillotine.* He held the bird higher, as high as he could, and watched as the last drops of blood oozed from the severed neck and dripped down onto the carpet of leaves underfoot.

Reverently, he placed it down on top of the stump, walked a few yards back into the trees, unzipped, and relieved himself. He was just zipping back up when he heard someone approaching from the west. He frowned. *Who the hell can that be? Bloody dangerous wandering around in the forest during turkey season. Silly son of a....* "What the hell? Hey... hey don't point that thing at me. That's how people get killed."

"Hmmm. Yes. That's true. Hi, Peter."

"What are you doing here?"

"Looking for you, of course. Where are the others?"

"Still out there somewhere. They'll be along in a minute."

"Hey, lucky you. You got one. Clean shot, too. Nice one."

"Lucky? Nah," he said, backing away slightly. "Technique. It's all about technique. Good woodcraft and technique. And, what are you doing? I asked you to point that thing somewhere else."

"You really are one smug son of a bitch, aren't you, Peter? Get down on your knees and beg, you bastard."

Peter Nicholson looked at the shotgun, now pointed at his chest. *"What?* What the hell are you talking about?"

"I'm talking about killing you, Peter. Now do as I say." The muzzle of the gun twitched, the way it did when someone put their finger on the trigger.

"You... you can't be serious."

"Oooh." The word was drawn out. Savored. "I'm serious. Now, we can do it the easy way, or I can blow your damned head off, like you did that bird's."

Nicholson put his hands in the air and began to back away.

"Stop, you piece a' shit." The gun swung up toward his face.

"Okay, okay." Nicholson stopped and dropped to his knees, his hands high over his head. "Why... why are you doing this? I haven't ever...."

"Oh yes you have. One way or another, you've screwed over everybody you've ever come in contact with, and me... well, you know why *I'm* going to kill you, don't you Peter?"

Nicholson stared at the muzzle of the gun. It didn't waver. "But...."

"No buts. You're a blight, Peter, a goddamn disease. Well, no more. It stops, right here and now.... God, how I despise you!"

"You can't... you *can't*. You—you—you won't get away with it."

"Hah! We'll see, but I don't have time to argue the point." The muzzle of the gun came up just slightly.

"No!" Nicholson shouted. He shoved his hands out in front of him and jerked backward just as—

The blast blew him backward and sideways and then down to the forest floor. The wound didn't look like much, not through the fabric of the quilted vest he was wearing. But the wad of number four shot had torn through flesh and bone and heart muscle... and it didn't even hurt.

"Oh," Peter Nicholson said. "Oh."

THE KILLER STOOD over the body, looked around, took careful note of the scene, then set the gun down and began to quickly rearrange things. First, the dead man was rolled over onto his stomach, then aligned west to east along the path, facing toward the trailhead. The legs were repositioned so that the feet were wide apart, the right arm folded underneath the body, the left arm positioned so that it pointed along the trail.

The killer stepped back, then forward again to adjust the position of the head, tilting it so that the chin and nose were in the dirt, and then stood back again, surveyed the scene once more, nodded approvingly, stepped forward again, picked up Nicholson's shotgun from the stump, opened the breach, checked it, noted the two live rounds therein, closed it again and fired one shot into the air, then stepped carefully to the right side of the body, lifted it, and slid the muzzle of the gun under it so that it rested close to the wound, the stock pointing down the trail. The dead man was now lying on the gun.

Smiling, the killer untied the shoelace of Nicholson's right boot and arranged the two tails so that they could easily be seen, then stepped back again and looked carefully around the scene, making sure everything was as it should be, that there were no loose ends.... *Except for the shoelaces, hah!* The killer smiled. *You really should have been more careful, Peter. Tripping and falling on your gun like that.... What's that? Someone's coming.*

The killer looked quickly around, bent down and grabbed the gun, then ran back along the trail for a short distance, stepped off into the forest, and pushed through the undergrowth for a hundred yards or so, found a secluded spot, and settled down to wait.

2

MONDAY, JANUARY 9, 2017

I was feeling particularly pleased with myself as I drove down Scenic Highway that morning. It would be my first day back at the office after an extended honeymoon and vacation. For six of the eight weeks I'd been away, Amanda and I had sailed the Caribbean in a chartered sailboat—a forty-four-foot catamaran named the *Lady May*—and the other two weeks I'd spent sorting out the Martan family murders on Calypso Key in the US Virgin Islands. Now I was back and itching to get to work.

Amanda, my new wife, had already headed into town, to Channel 7, in the hopes of getting her old job back. She'd quit as their lead anchor a few months before the wedding, ostensibly to reconstruct, renovate, and decorate my—now our—new home on Lookout Mountain. She'd enjoyed not having to work for a while, but... well, eventually she started to miss the job, and I couldn't say I blamed her. I felt exactly the same.

And so it was that I walked into my offices on Georgia Avenue that January Monday morning to wild applause from my gathered crew.... I'm Harry Starke, by the way and, in case you didn't know, a private investigator and reluctant celebrity. I own and operate Harry Starke Investigations, and very successfully too, I might add. But to continue....

The clapping and hooting and dirty comments from Bob Ryan, my number two, only enhanced my good mood. I was glad to be back among my friends and ready to begin work. And so, the greetings and backslapping over and done with, I had everyone move into the conference room for the first weekly meeting I'd attended in more than two months.

Jacque, my PA, and Bob had run things while I was away, and for the next hour they filled me in on what had been happening: old cases and new, and how they were being handled. And, as the meeting dragged on, I became more and more aware that I was about to become a victim of my own success, that my staff was well able to run the company without me.

As I sat back and listened, first to Jacque, then to Bob, then Tim, Ronnie Hall, and finally Heather Stillwell, my second lead investigator, I was overcome by a sinking feeling that things would never again be as they had; my fledgling brood had found their wings, and I was all but redundant.

And so I listened, and I absorbed. I nodded, shook my head as needed, and I even asked questions, until finally....

"Okay," I said, leaning forward and folding my arms on the table—my wounded arm had fully healed by then. "Well done everyone. I knew I was leaving the agency in good hands. Thank you, but what the hell am I supposed to do now?"

"It's just good to have you back, boss," Bob said, and there was a murmur of agreement all around the table.

"And I'm glad to be back, but it seems like you have everything well in hand." I looked at each of them; they looked back, most of them smiling. "Okay. I get it. Jacque, you and Bob, my office. Let's get coffee first.... What?" I asked, as Bob shook his head.

"Can't, Harry. I have an appointment in—" he looked at his watch "—thirty minutes. Sorry. Gotta go. Can't be late." He got up from the table, gathered his stuff, grinned at me, and walked out of the room, closing the door behind him.

Well hell. "Jacque. My office. Now."

My office had that... that... unlived-in smell, or maybe feel, about it. It wasn't cold, at least not in the usual sense of the word, but it was... I dunno, vacant-ish?

"Sit," I told Jacque. "I'll turn the logs on. Cheer the place up a bit." I rotated the gas tap and pushed the igniter; there was a whoosh, and happy flames danced around the synthetic logs—cheery, but not the real thing. *Oh well, better than nothing, I guess.*

"Talk to me, Jacque," I said, sliding into my leather throne behind the desk—I was surprised to see my computer was already up and running.

"About what? We just got trew with telling you about

arl the work and cases," she said, playing up her usually much softer accent. She was teasing me.

I nodded, sighed, looked at her over the polished acreage that was my desk and said, wistfully, "Jacque, is there nothing at all for me to do? You and Bob... you're doing a great job of running things, but hell, I'm not a figurehead, damn it. I need to work. Isn't there something I can get my teeth into?"

She smiled at me. "But you said, before you left to go gallivantin' arl over the Caribbean, that this was what you wanted, that you were going to hand over the day-to-day running of the business to me and Bob. We took you at your word. Now you're complainin' about it?"

"No, I'm just... surprised and... hell, Jacque. I feel like I'm not needed anymore. It's—it's not nice, damn it."

"Oh, don't you go worryin'. It will be fine. There will be somethin' for you soon, I'm sure. In the meantime, I'll bring you the mail. Maybe there'll be something there for you." She paused. "Are we all done then? Because I have things to do, a company to run." She was laughing as she said it, but I'm not sure how funny it was, at least to me.

"Yeah, go on. Get outa here. Bring me the mail... wait. Isn't that Leslie's job?" Leslie Rhodes was one of my clerks, Margo Tyler being the other.

"It is, but I'm sure she won't mind you helping her out." More laughter.

"Go on. Get out of here."

And she did, with a swish of her hips and a swirl of her skirt.

I was left in what had become almost an alien environment, a vast, open room with no one but me in it, and me with nothing but a half cup of lukewarm coffee. Nothing to think about, nothing to do but twiddle my thumbs, which is pretty much what I did for at least five minutes. *Jeez, I always have something to think about. I wonder how Amanda's getting on....*

So I called her to find out.

"Hey you," I said when she answered. "I hope you're having a better day than I am. They've just about taken over here. I have absolutely nothing, and I do mean *nothing*, to do."

"Oh come on, Harry. It can't be that bad."

"*Yeah.* It can and it is. How about you? Did they give you your job back?"

"They did, but I won't start until the first of February. What are you doing now?"

"I told you. *Nothing!*"

"So how about you take me to lunch?"

"Ummm, well. Okay."

"Whoa, don't sound so enthusiastic."

"It's not that. I just... feel like I'm at loose ends. I'm not used to it, and I don't like it. Yes. Sure. Let's go to lunch. The Public House okay?"

"Hmmm, I suppose."

"*Now* who sounds enthusiastic?"

"No. It's fine. It's just that it's usually so busy."

"Give them a call and see if that room off to the side is available."

"Done. If not, well, I'll just have to suck it up. See you in thirty. Bye."

"Yeah, bye." I disconnected and called Kate Gazzara, my one-time, now sometime partner, a homicide lieutenant in the Major Crimes Unit at the Chattanooga PD. We go back a long way, Kate and I... but that's a whole 'nother story, and one for another time. Anyway, she and I had solved the Calypso Key murders some two months ago when I was supposed to be on my honeymoon: she and the rest of my friends were in attendance, and—

"Hello, Harry," she said when the call connected. "You back in the saddle again?"

I almost rolled my eyes. "Not hardly. They've just about done away with my job while I was gone. I feel like an unwanted guest."

She laughed. "Yeah, I heard. I wouldn't get bent out of shape about it; they're just trying to get you to take it a little easy, is all."

"Easy? You have to be kidding me. I'm forty-four, not seventy-four. I'm sitting here staring at the ceiling and drinking enough coffee to kill a horse."

"I hear you. Hey. You'll figure it out. In the meantime, how was your trip? Amanda fed up with you yet?"

"She's not, no, and the trip was wonderful. But listen. I just wanted to touch base, let you know I was back. Can you talk?"

"Well, I'm pretty busy now, but how 'bout you call me this evening."

"That's fine."

"Then have a good one, Harry," she said, and disconnected.

I sighed, tossed the phone down on my desk. Then I went back to twiddling my thumbs.

3

MONDAY, JANUARY 9, 3:00 P.M

By three o'clock that afternoon, I'd had enough. I'd arrived back from lunch at around one thirty, done the rounds, annoyed everyone in the place, even dragged Tim kicking and screaming out of his cyber world, all to no avail. It wasn't that they didn't want me there; there was just nothing for me to do. So there I was, back in my own office, packing my laptop, iPhone, and what was left of a Cadbury chocolate bar into my briefcase, about to head on back up the mountain when Jacque came in.

"So," she said, closing the door behind her, "I have a woman out there who says she needs a little help. She asked for you by name. You want to talk to her?"

I screwed up my face. I was skeptical.

"Any idea what she wants?"

"She wouldn't say."

"Well, what do you think? Divorce case? Cheating

husband? If so, no; I don't want to talk to her. Give it to Heather."

"I don't think so. She's an older woman, looks... I don't know, affluent? I think you should at least see what she needs. You did say you wanted—"

"Okay, okay, I know what I said. Show her in. I'll give her five minutes."

She nodded, backed out of the door, and returned a few seconds later. "Mrs. Helen Nicholson."

"Mrs. Nicholson," I said to the woman. "Come on in and please sit down," And she did, in one of the two guest chairs in front of my desk. "What can I do for you?"

She didn't answer right away. Instead, she looked at me over the desk. I had the distinct feeling she was sizing me up in some way.

She was indeed, as Jacque had put it, affluent, and I was surprised I didn't know her... or did I? The name Nicholson did tinkle a bell or two somewhere in the farthest reaches of my subconscious. She was obviously one of Chattanooga's moneyed elite. The gray Burberry overcoat and matching woolen dress must have cost a bundle.

She looked to be in her early sixties, slim, graying hair, and quite lovely—and not just because of the expensive work she'd had done on her face.

"You're trying to figure out where you know me from, aren't you, Mr. Starke."

The voice was low, confident, refined, and English; the smile entrancing. She reminded me somewhat of Lauren Bacall in her later years.

"Do I know you?" I asked.

"Not personally, no. I do know your father, August, quite well, though he knows nothing about this visit. Lovely man, your father. Rose is a lucky woman."

I nodded, though nothing she'd said made her look any more familiar. I decided on the direct approach.

"So why *are* you here, Mrs. Nicholson? Is it your husband?" I smiled at her. "Do you want to have him followed?"

"Hardly. I know you have a reputation for getting results, but I think even you might have difficulties pulling that one off. Chester passed away five years ago. No, it's my son I want to talk to you about."

She crossed her legs, adjusted her skirt, and folded her hands in her lap. She carried no pocketbook or clutch, and if she had a cell phone with her it wasn't evident.

"Your son?" I leaned back in my chair, rested my elbows on the arms, steepled my fingers to my lips, and waited for her to continue.

"My son, yes, Peter. He died in a hunting accident almost fifteen years ago, in May of 2002. Well. They *said* it was an accident, but I know it wasn't. He was murdered."

Now she had my attention.

"Murdered?"

She nodded, clasped her hands together, looked down at them, then up at me.

"Yes, Mr. Starke. Shot through the heart while out hunting turkey. They said he tripped and fell on his gun.

I didn't think so then and I don't think so now. And I want you to look into his death."

"What makes you think it wasn't an accident, and why now?"

"His death was... too convenient. Too many people benefited from it, but it's more than that. Where his guns were concerned, Peter was a very careful man. He habitually carried his shotgun in the break position, either over his shoulder or under his arm; now and then he would carry it with the breach closed, by his side, but not often. I know. I used to shoot with him, once in a while. It wasn't a cardinal rule, but unless he was in a shooting position, the breach would have been open."

She paused for a moment, looked down at her hands, then continued.

"As for why now.... I've been trying to get the case reopened since the day it was closed more than fourteen years ago. I have, over the years, managed to persuade two police chiefs—including Chief Johnston—two sheriffs, and two district attorneys to look into it, all to no avail. After cursory glances at the case, the consensus among law enforcement is that it was an accident. So you see, you're my last hope. Will you help me?"

"I don't know if I can. If they all say...."

"Yes. I know what you're going to say. If it walks like a duck...."

I nodded.

"Well, thank you for your time." She started to rise. "I'm sorry I bothered you."

"Whoa. I didn't say I wouldn't try; just that I didn't know if I could help you. Please, sit down. Let's talk."

Reluctantly, she resumed her seat. I placed my elbows back on the chair, fingers to my lips, and looked at her. There was a certain defiance about her. She sat bolt upright, her back not touching the chair, head tilted slightly to one side, hands clasped together in her lap.

"Tell me about it," I said, "but before you do, would you like some coffee?"

"That would be nice. I take it black, please."

I picked up the phone and asked Margo to bring two cups. She did.

I took my digital recorder from my desk drawer, turned it on, and placed it between us in the center of the desk.

"So, let's begin with the personal stuff," I said. "You're obviously English, right?"

"Yes. We came to the United States in 1987. My husband, Chester, was a heart surgeon. He had been offered a position at what is now CHI Memorial Hospital. Peter was eighteen at the time."

Hmmm, then you're a lot older than you look— seventy, seventy-one, maybe.

"I'm sixty-nine, Mr. Starke," she said with a wry smile. "That was what you were thinking, wasn't it?"

"You could tell what I was thinking?" I smiled at her.

"I'm a woman. Of course I could tell."

I simply lowered and shook my head. "Please continue, Mrs. Nicholson."

"Oh, please call me Helen." She paused, then went

on. "My son was an investment broker, though perhaps not the most successful in his field. He specialized in high-yield instruments and... well, he... he... made several mistakes." She paused, picked up her coffee, sipped, and looked at me over the rim of the cup.

I waited. *High yield? That means high risk. And I wonder what she means by "mistakes." Bad investments, bad management.... Rip off....*

"He liked to golf and he loved to hunt," she continued, breaking into my thoughts. "Hunting was his passion."

She pursed her lips, then sighed through her nose, irritably. "He was a member of the country club, as was his father. He had friends, Mr. Starke. Lots of friends, but he wasn't a popular man, and I say that as his mother. He was arrogant, even pompous, argumentative, and he was never wrong about anything. A least, that's what he believed. He loved his wife—though why, I have no idea —she was, and still is, a first-class bitch. I'm sure you know her. She's remarried. Mary Ann Warren."

Oh yes, I know Mary Ann, and her husband.

I nodded. "Yes, I have a passing acquaintance with her and Judge Warren." *Sheesh, now there's an understatement.*

"Yes, well, Ellis was with Peter when he died. I should say, he was there, but not exactly with him, at least that's what he claims."

"So tell me about it, the accident."

She looked sharply at me. "It was no accident, Mr. Starke."

"Yes, ma'am, I understand. Please continue."

"There were four of them: my son, Peter, Ellis Warren, Heath Myers, and Alex Harrison."

Oh hell, here we go. Trouble!

"They were on a turkey hunt in Prentice Cooper. They'd split up, so they said, and were spread out over a fairly wide, designated area. Each had a spot of his own. These were issued by lottery.

"It was late afternoon. Apparently they'd just about finished for the day and were wrapping things up when they—Ellis, Heath, and Alex—heard first one gunshot and then, a few minutes later, another. They said they didn't think anything of it. That they each thought it was one of the others taking his final shots.

"Anyway, they were returning to a prearranged location at the trailhead to meet up when they found Peter facedown on the trail, dead from a gunshot wound to the heart. Heath Myers was the first to arrive on the scene. He was quickly followed by Ellis and Alex. It appeared that Peter had tripped and fallen on his gun. The emergency services were called, of course, including the medical examiner at the time, Dr. Bowden, and Sheriff Hands with a couple of detectives. The sheriff's office conducted an investigation—and I use that word, 'investigation,' lightly. Dr. Bowden confirmed that Peter was dead and recorded the cause as accidental. The sheriff took him at his word and closed the case. That's it. Oh... no, it's not; not quite. Warren married my son's wife less than two years after his death. They'd been having an affair for years. Does that not tell you something?"

"Hmmm," I said, shaking my head. "It's interesting, I agree. Warren, Myers, and Harrison," I said, more to myself than to her. "Whew." *Whew? The three horsemen....*

She smiled. "You know them, then?"

"I do indeed. Professionally and socially. Warren is a senior circuit court judge, Alex Harrison is an assistant United States attorney, and Myers is a tort lawyer, in the same line of business as my father. They've run up against each other more than once, and they don't get along."

I leaned back in my chair and stared up at the chandelier. *You don't need this, Harry. It could get really ugly. Tell her it's a lost cause and get her out of here....* But then: *Lost cause, huh? I wonder. Warren, he's one nasty son of a bitch... and so's Harrison. Hmmm, might be fun to jerk their chains a little. Ah, but.... Sheesh, Harry, you've got nothing else to do.... Yep, and I do love a cold one, beer or case. Let's do it.*

I let my chair tilt forward again, clasped my hands together on top of the desk, and looked hard at her. She held my gaze until finally she said, "Well? Will you help me?"

"Why me, Mrs. Nicholson?"

"That's easy. You have clout enough in this town that you can't be ignored. You can make people take notice. So, will you help me?"

"I will, but I can make no promises.... No, no, let me finish. You need to understand that if I agree to do this, it will cause problems for both of us. These are some very important people I'll be dealing with and they won't thank me for dragging up the past. And, it's possible it really was just an accident."

"I understand. Let's talk about your fees. I've waited a long time for this. Tell me how it works, please."

"I charge $225 per hour, plus expenses, which can be extensive. I'll also require a $10,000 retainer. Any unused balance will be returned to you. Okay?" She took a checkbook and pen from a pocket in the coat. Opened it, laid it on the desk, and began to write. She signed it with a flourish, tore it from the book, and handed to me across the desk. I looked at it, noted the amount, and looked up at her in surprise.

"I've made it out for $25,000. I want you to work exclusively for me until you've solved it, one way or the other."

Hah, how convenient. Right now I have nothing to do but work for her.

I looked at the check, nodded, slid it to one side, took my iPad and stylus from the desk drawer, and prepared to take notes.

"So let's get started then. I need to ask you some questions." I picked up the recorder, made sure it was on, and then lay it back on the desk.

"I need the date and time of the incident, please."

"Friday, May 3, 2002, at approximately four o'clock in the afternoon."

"Do you know exactly where it took place?"

"I do, and I would be happy to take you there, if it would help."

"It might. I'll think about it. Who was the investigating officer?"

"There were two of them. Sheriff's officers. Lieutenant Wade Brewer—he died two years ago—and Sergeant Ron Fowler. He's retired. He's in poor health, so I understand."

I made a note of the names.

"I talked to both of them," she said. "Brewer was very reluctant to see me, and when he did, he had little to say, but I got the impression that he never agreed with the finding that it was an accident. Fowler was more forthcoming. He said he was sure that it wasn't an accident, but he was pressured by the sheriff, and others he wouldn't name, and so had no option but to take the low road. Those three were influential men, even back then. I talked with Fowler several times; he always said that there were things at the site that didn't add up, but he was just a detective then and pretty low on the pecking order."

"I take it there was an autopsy?"

"There was. I have a copy. I'll scan it and e-mail it to you."

"You didn't bring it with you?"

She smiled. "No. I'm sorry. I really didn't think you would take it on."

I smiled back at her. "Lucky you, maybe. So, if you have that, you know the exact cause of death."

She nodded. "Yes. He died from a 12-gauge shotgun blast to the heart. They say he died instantly. It was, so

I'm told, a contact wound incurred when he fell on the gun, which is nonsense."

"What type of gun was it, do you know?"

"Yes, of course. I still have it. It's an old Browning 12-gauge, and actually quite valuable."

Hmmm, I wonder if I'm wasting my time.

"I don't like that look on your face, Mr. Starke. What are you thinking?"

I shook my head. "Nothing. Just churning some stuff around. Nothing for you to worry about. I think I have what I need for now. If you could get that autopsy report to me as soon as possible... well. Can you do it this afternoon?"

"Yes, of course. I'll send it as soon as I get home. Is there anything else you need?"

"I'd like to take a look at the gun."

"Of course. I'll drop it off early in the morning?"

"Yes. I'll be here by eight thirty. Shall we say nine?"

She nodded.

"Maybe," I said, "if you have time, we'll go look at the site. I doubt there's anything I can learn from it after all this time; I'd just like to familiarize myself with it, get a feel for it."

"Yes. I have time. I can take you to the exact spot."

"Very well, then. I'll see you tomorrow morning. In the meantime...."

"Yes, the autopsy report. I won't forget."

We chatted for a couple minutes more, and then I showed her out, grabbed a double cup of Dark Italian

Roast, and returned to my office. On the way, I signaled for Jacque to join me.

"So," she said, sitting down in the seat recently vacated by Helen Nicholson. "I take it you have a case to work. You want to tell me about it?"

I sat, set my coffee down, picked up the check, glanced at it, and then handed it to her.

"Nice one," she said, laying it down on the desk. "What do you have to do to earn it? Sell your body?"

I laughed, then filled her in on what I knew about the case. When I mentioned Judge Warren, she frowned and shook her head.

"You know what you're getting into?" she asked. "From what little I know of the judge, he can be... a hardass?"

"Oh yeah. That's Warren, but it won't be the first run-in I've had with him. Fortunately, I too have friends in high places, but it's not just him. Harrison is a federal prosecutor; that's going to be a tough nut to crack. Myers, not so much. He's a total ass, but he has no official standing like the other two."

"And if what Helen Nicholson says is true," Jacque said, "it's likely that one of the three murdered her son."

I nodded, sat back in my chair, hoisted my feet up onto the desk, cradled my cup in both hands, and stared up at the ceiling.

"It's not going to be easy, Jacque. The case is almost fifteen years cold. Much of the evidence, if there ever was any, is long gone. There's an autopsy report. I can have Doc Sheddon go through that with me. There are bound to be photos and videos somewhere, maybe even news footage. I'll ask Amanda to check Channel 7's archives; they'll cooperate. It will be a hell of a story for them if it comes to anything. The lead detective is deceased; I'm not sure about Bowden, the ME.... I dunno, and I won't until I can start digging."

"Sounds like it's right up your alley," she said. "What can I do to help?"

I handed her the recorder. "The first thing you can do is make copies of the interview and have Margo transcribe it, and that autopsy report should be here by now...." I clicked into my e-mail. It was. "Then," I continued, "hmmm. Why don't you give the sheriff's office a call, see if they have anything left over from the investigation? They should. Peter Nicholson was an important personality here in the Scenic City. I vaguely remember the coverage. I was still a cop at the time; just made sergeant. His death was all over the news, a one-day wonder. If the sheriff's people do have anything, ask if we can have access to it.... No, no. let's not do that. Let's not give 'em the chance to 'lose' it. What time is it?" I looked at my watch. It was almost four thirty.

"Tell you what. If you have a few minutes free, let's you and I go on over there. If there is anything, I'd like to get my hands on it before the word gets leaked to Warren and he puts a damper on it, or worse."

4

MONDAY JANUARY 9, 4:00 P.M

I t's rare that you can walk into the Hamilton County Sheriff's Department and be granted an audience with the man himself. That day, however, we got lucky. Not only was he available, he also agreed to see us.

Sheriff Steve Walker was an unlikely pick for the post, most notably because, unlike his predecessor Israel Hands, he was an exceedingly likeable individual, imposing, handsome, with a sharp wit and an acid tongue.

"Harry Starke." He all but shouted it as he came around from behind his desk, his hand extended for me to shake, which I did. "And who's this young lady?"

"Jacque is my PA, Steve. Jacque, say hello to Sheriff Walker."

She did.

"So, I hear you've decided to settle down at last," he said, resuming his seat behind the desk. "Sit down, sit down, both of you. Take a load off."

"The time was right, I guess...."

"And to Amanda Cole, no less. That broke a few hearts around here, let me tell you. Jeez, I have to wonder though—what the hell does she see in you?"

"Must be my good looks and charming personality," I said dryly. "Steve, I need a favor."

"Ah, and there's that charming personality. Whadda ya need?"

"Do you remember the Peter Nicholson case? It was back in May of 2002."

"Oh yeah, course. Nicholson's mother's been in here a few times. He fell on his gun and shot himself, right?"

"Well, that was the verdict at the time."

He leaded forward, frowning. "You sayin' it was something else, Harry?"

"Nope, but his mother came by to see me too. I agreed to look into it, hence my visit to you. You say she's been in to see you?"

"Yep. A couple of times—three, in fact."

"And?"

"And nothing. The ME said it was an accident. That's it. I told her so."

"Did you look into it at all?" I asked.

"I didn't. Well, I looked at the records, but Hands did all the work, back in '02. He agreed with the ME. Accident."

"And... you didn't look at it yourself. Come on Steve. You know what Israel Hands was. If he said it was an accident, that would be a good enough reason to make sure that's exactly what it was, or wasn't."

He shrugged. "So you say, but this is a busy office. You know that. I have better things to do than go chasing shadows. The medical examiner said it was an accident, and I had no cause to think otherwise."

I nodded. He was right.

He sat still for a moment, staring at me, slowly shaking his head.

"Do you have any idea what you're getting into, Harry?" he asked quietly.

I didn't answer. I just grinned at him.

"As I recall, there were three friends with Nicholson that day. Today, those three are listed among the top ten movers and shakers in the city. You sure you want to go head to head with them?"

"Movers and shakers they may be, but they're people, just like you and me and, like you and me, they're not above the law. Steve, I know all three of them, socially and professionally. I don't like any of them. They are all members of the country club. My father has butted heads with Myers several times, and he's always come out ahead. Me? I've run headfirst into Warren a dozen or more times. He hates my guts. Harrison... ah, not so much, but he's a nasty son of a bitch. Steve, you were with the department in 2002. It was high profile. So what was your take on it?"

"Harry, I was a rookie deputy back then. I'd been on the force less than a year. I wasn't involved in the investigation at all." He paused. I waited.

"Well," I said, finally, "go on."

"I dunno, Harry. There was some talk about Warren and Mary Ann...."

"Yes, Nicholson's mother told me. They married less than two years later. What was the gossip? Were they were having an affair? If so, that could be a motive."

"I don't know. It was just talk, Harry. You know how it is. You were part of the department once; the place is a gossip mill, for God's sake. And anyway, as I said, I had nothing to do with it. Wade Brewer ran that investigation. Him and Ron Fowler."

"Yeah, I heard that too. How about records? It's only been fifteen years. You still have them, right?"

He nodded. "Thanks to Mrs. Nicholson's persistence. They should have been dumped years ago, and would have been if not for her."

"So, how about you let me have 'em for a couple of days and—"

"Harry, I don't know. Accident or not.... It gets out...."

"It gets out and nothing. You just said they should have been dumped, so what's the problem? Come on, Steve. I need this. I'll owe you, okay?"

He stared at me across the desk. I could feel Jacque squirming in the seat next to me, but I never took my eyes off him, not for a second. Finally, he broke, glanced away, and shook his head.

"I know I'm going to regret this," he said, with a sigh and a shake of his head. He rose to his feet. "Stay here. I'll be back."

And he was, less than five minutes later, bearing a

large cardboard box and a black plastic bag; both were taped and tagged.

"Here. Take it," he said, handing the box to me and the bag to Jacque. "Now get the hell out of here. Oh, and yeah. You *do* owe me."

And that's what we did. Less than five minutes later we were back in my office. We dumped the contents of the plastic bag and the box on my desk. I took a quick peek inside the bag. It was full of evidence bags containing items of clothing: jeans, shirts, a quilted vest, a ball cap, a pair of hunting boots: obviously the clothes that Nicholson had been wearing when he died. Next, I looked inside the box and noted a number of files and a smaller box containing some odds and ends, notably spent shotgun shells and a number of 8mm video tapes, each in separate, labeled evidence bags.

"It's too late to get started on this," I told Jacque. "Go home. We'll do it tomorrow morning."

5

MONDAY, JANUARY 9, 6:00 P.M

The ride up Lookout Mountain that evening was a pleasant one. It was already dark and the lights of the city were spread out on my left like a jeweled carpet, and I was in an almost euphoric mood. I had a case to work, albeit a cold one. *And cold cases, like good brandy, mature with age.*

It wasn't just that, though. I was looking forward to a nice dinner and an evening of marital bliss. I was to be disappointed on both grounds.

Amanda's not actually a bad cook, but somehow the pot roast she'd prepared didn't quite work out. The bread was hard—I could have used it to patch the crumbling perimeter walls—and the peach cobbler had come from a freezer at the local supermarket. Only the wine was palatable, and that was because it came from my own private stock.

The evening of marital bliss turned into a serious

discussion of the Nicholson case, which Amanda remembered vividly, and was not wild about me taking.

"Judge Ellis Warren, Alex Harrison, and Heath Myers.... You don't for one minute think they're going to talk to you, do you, any of them?" she asked. "All three of them, are the... the... the worst... oh I'm going to say it. They are three of the finest criminal minds in the tristate area, and I'm not talking jurisprudence. They are damned crooks, all three of them, and so are the people who work for them. Damn it, Harry. You know how it is in this town. Everybody knows everybody. There was even talk that Warren was—and maybe still is—involved with Little Billy Harper. Harry, please think very carefully about this."

She was seated across from me at the table. She'd eaten almost nothing, and she looked worried. Very worried.

I laid down my dessert fork, pushed away my untouched plate of cobbler, and reached for my glass.

"Honey, I know those three better than anyone, and you're right about them, but if one of them... or all of them together killed Peter Nicholson, I have to find out and bring them to justice. Besides," I said, almost as an afterthought, "I need something to do, and this is right up my street. It has all the makings: a mysterious death, three really bad characters... and Lauren Bacall." I grinned at her as I said it.

She stared at me, eyes wide, and then said, "Okay.... Lauren Bacall. Do tell." And I did, and she smiled.

"So now you think you're Sam Spade." She laughed.

"Sometimes, Harry, you're just too much. I'm going to bed." She got up from the table and walked to the door. "If you need me, just whistle. You do know how to whistle, don't you, Harry?"

"Yeah, yeah, I just put my lips together and blow. Now get outa here and leave me to think a little longer, and then...."

"No chance, Sam. I am not in the mood."

"All right, all right. But hey, one more thing before you go. The Nicholson death was pretty high profile back in the day. Channel 7 should have all sorts of stuff in the archives, right?"

"Maybe. I'll take a look."

"Okay... when?"

She heaved a sigh. "Tomorrow?" And she left me there alone with my thoughts, the remains of the meal, and what was left of the wine. I sighed and began to clean up the table.

Nice one, Amanda.

6

TUESDAY JANUARY 10, 8:00 A.M

I got to the office early the following morning. In fact, I was the first one in the door. I fired up the gas logs in my office, turned on all the lights to brighten up the place, and then went back to the outer office to get coffee. I selected a large ceramic mug and filled it with two nine-ounce shots of Dark Italian Roast. The Keurig had just finished its second cycle when Jacque walked in, followed by Bob. I removed my mug from the machine and stood back and watched as first Jacque then Bob repeated the process. I left Bob to do his thing and steered Jacque into my office.

The box, containing what little evidence there was, was still where I'd left it on my desk, right next to the plastic bag containing Peter's clothing. So I dropped into my seat and began to dig through it; Jacque sat opposite.

First I flipped quickly through the photos, crime scene and autopsy, and then handed them to her to look at. They were all standard stuff: well shot, and they told the story, as far as was possible. Next, I scanned the incident report, also standard stuff—short, plain, and to the point: the man had tripped over his bootlace and fallen on his gun. The autopsy report I set aside for later. The smaller box contained a typewritten inventory of the contents of Nicholson's pockets, several evidence baggies containing spent and live shells, a small plastic bottle containing, so its label told me, 147 shotgun pellets—number four shot. There were also nine Sony Hi8 Handycam 8mm video tapes, each individually bagged and labeled.

I picked up the phone and punched the buttons that would connect me with Tim and asked him to join us.

Tim Clarke is an anomaly. He's my computer geek and extremely expensive—he earns every penny of his salary and much more, but he has an annoying habit of buying expensive equipment for the company and not telling me about it, his idea being that, if he needs it, so do I. He handles all things Internet, including operating and maintaining the company website. His more mundane duties include running background checks and skip searches. He can find people, addresses, phone numbers, you name it, no matter where they might be. He's a geek in every sense of the word: tall, skinny, glasses, twenty-six years old, perhaps the most intelligent person I've ever met, and arguably the most useful and effective tool in my bag.

He entered my office loaded to the gills: laptop in the crook of his arm, iPad under the other arm, stylus between his teeth, an overfull cup of coffee in his free hand that he laid down on my mahogany desk, slopping the stuff all over it.

"Whoops," he said, spitting the stylus into his now free hand. "Sorry, boss. I'll get some paper towels."

"No need, Tim," I said dryly, taking a fistful of tissues from the box Jacque insists on putting on my desk and wiping the offending liquid away. "What the hell is all that stuff for?"

"Well, you never know," he said, taking the seat next to Jacque. "It's always best to be prepared, I say. I might need the laptop for—"

"Yeah, yeah, I get it. But you won't need any of it."

I reached into the box and took out the incident report. "These three men, and the victim. I want to know all there is to know about them, from grade school through today. I want five copies and I want them by two o'clock this afternoon. Can you manage that?"

He gave me a wry look that said I should know better than to ask such a stupid question. And I should have, but still.

He nodded. "Anything else?"

"No. I'm going out. When I get back, I need you ready to go to work. We'll meet here in my office at two. Okay?"

He grinned, got to his feet, somehow gathered his stuff together again—this time managing not to spill the coffee—and left. Jacque did have to get up and open the door for him, though.

When she sat down again, I looked at her across my desk, hesitating for a moment. She was wearing a dark gray business suit, and three-inch heels. Hardly the right outfit for what I had in mind. "How busy are you, Jacque? I need you to turn yourself loose for two or three hours. Can Leslie run things for a little while?"

She looked at me. There was a strange light in her eyes. "Yes.... She... can manage without me. Things are pretty much together. Why?"

"Good. I'd like you to come with me and Helen Nicholson to the scene this morning. There's something bothering me about what I'm seeing in these photos. She's also bringing the gun that killed her son. I'd like to do a little reconstructing. You up for it?"

"Am I up for it?"

I grinned at her. Her Jamaican accent always came out front and center when she was excited.

"What you tink? Of course I am."

"Good. We're going to need some luminol. There's not much chance we'll find blood after all these years, but it's not unheard of. See if we have some Bluestar; that's about the only stuff that might bring it up. Can I leave that to you? Oh, and we'll also need a small tarp, a measuring tape, and one of the Nikons."

"You got it. An' I'll need to change clothes," she said, and went off to do it.

I opened the plastic bag and took out the packages one by one. They were labeled, but the seals were broken —the chain of custody, if there ever officially had been one, was no more. Each bag contained a single item: a white undershirt, a red and black flannel shirt, and a dark gray Arc'teryx vest; the fronts were stiff with dried blood.

The rubber hunting boots were L.L.Bean, the socks were thick wool, the white ball cap was by Ahead, and a pair of white boxers and a pair of Arc'teryx outdoor pants completed the ensemble.

I laid the undershirt, shirt, and vest side by side on the desk. Each piece had a hole in it approximately one and a half inches in diameter. Without bothering to put the items together, I could see that the holes matched up, about four inches down from the top of the left shirt collar and about an inch and a half from the vest's zipper. I looked closely at the hole in the vest. If there was gunshot residue present, I couldn't see it. It might have been masked by the dried blood, which itself was beginning to powder.

That will have to be tested.

I placed the items back in their respective bags, looked at my watch, and then put the evidence bags back in the plastic bag. It was 8:40—time enough for another cup of coffee.

IT WAS JUST after nine when Helen Nicholson walked into my outer office, a soft leather shotgun case under her arm. I greeted her, took the case from her, and unzipped it.

The gun, a 1968 Belgian Browning Superposed, over/under 12-gauge was, itself, encased in a large paper evidence bag; its seals were still intact, and the chain of custody list still intact—hers being the last name on it.

I took it from her and added my name to the list, Jacque initialing as witness to the change of custody. As I said earlier, the chain, if ever there really had been one, was no longer valid for anything else, but I did my stuff anyway. Habit, I guess. That done, I set the gun down on my desk; the seals would remain intact, at least for now. I wasn't sure what good that would do, but I wouldn't break them until I had to, and only then with witnesses present.

"So, you ready for a look at the site?" I asked Mrs. Nicholson.

She nodded. I looked at Jacque, now dressed in jeans, a sweater, and hiking boots; her hair was, the giant black Afro she liked to affect from time to time. I shook my head, smiled at her.

"What?"

"Nothing. You look great."

She pursed her lips, frowned, and glared at me. "You want me to go change?"

"Nope. Just grab a coat and let's go."

"Huh!"

I grabbed the Browning and went to the gun safe in the back office, where I deposited it and checked out my own Benelli 828U over/under 12-gauge shotgun; not quite the same as Peter's, but near enough for what I needed.

Jacque, now wearing a white, shiny, quilted jacket, had a camera slung over one shoulder and a large black backpack over the other. She gave Leslie a few last-minute instructions and we headed out into the parking lot. We dropped everything into the trunk of my Maxima and I nosed the car out through the security gates into the traffic on Georgia Avenue, turned right, then right again onto MLK, and finally right again onto Highway 27, and then headed across the river. Twenty minutes later we pulled into the parking lot of the TWRA's Forest Office. I always like to check in with the powers that be, and I had an idea these folks could be helpful. And I felt so even more when Captain John Evans, grinning like a fool, stepped out from behind his desk to greet me.

"Harry Friggin' Starke," he said, shoving his hand out. "Who the hell would have thought it?"

I smiled back at him—I couldn't help myself—and I shook his hand; a gorilla would have been proud of his grip. I'd known this man for more than half my life. We had gone to McCallie together, been the best of friends, but when we graduated, he went his way and I went mine. Every so often we'd bump into each other, sometimes at the club, sometime at that sordid little downtown joint, the Sorbonne. Today was a good day for me to meet up with him once more.

He looked at the women, and his face dropped. "Mrs. Nicholson." He shook his head. "You back again?"

"Yes, and I'll keep on coming back until I get justice for my son. You have no objections, I hope."

"No ma'am. In fact, I admire your spirit. After all these years...." He shook his head, looked at Jacque, and his lips broadened into a wide smile.

"And you are?" he asked, offering his hand.

"Jacque Hale, I'm...." She looked at me.

"Jacque is my personal assistant, my right arm in almost everything."

He nodded, released her hand. "You wanna tell me why you're here, Harry, and with Mrs. Nicholson?"

"Oh, I think you can guess."

"Yup. Ain't gonna do you no good though. Too many have already tried, and they all came up with the same answer: accident."

"Were you here back then, John?"

"Sure was. I was just an officer then, but I remember it well enough. In fact, I arrived at the scene just after they removed the body."

"You never told me that," Helen said, low-level anger in her voice.

"You're right, I didn't. Nor would I have now had it not been for Harry here. There was no need. I wasn't, and still ain't, a detective. Harry is though. You done good, Mrs. Nicholson. If anyone can get you some answers, it's him. Now—" he looked at me "—what can I do for you?"

"I'm going to visit the scene, if that's okay with you."

"Of course," he said, grabbing a heavy green uniform jacket from the rack by the door. "In fact, I'll go with you. Jake, you keep an eye on things. You heah?" The other man, significantly younger, looked up from his computer screen and nodded.

"Let's go," Evans said, as he held open the door for us. Once outside, he looked at the Maxima, shook his head, grinned, and said, "Good luck with that. It sure as hell ain't built for these forest roads.... You wanna take my truck?" He jerked his head in the direction of a muddy, green GMC 150 state truck. It was a king cab and I probably should have taken him up on the offer, but when I looked at the clothes the women were wearing, I knew it wasn't an option. Besides, all the gear was in my car.

"How about we follow," I said. "The Maxima has upgraded suspension; she can handle it. Just stop well short of the scene. I want to walk in."

He looked doubtfully at the Maxima's wheels, then at me. "What the hell are you expecting to find after all these years, Harry? You do know it's rained since then, right?"

He was being facetious, and I smiled for him. "Let's go, John. If you don't want to, I'm sure Mrs. Nicholson can show us the way."

He snorted. "I'm sure she could."

He ambled away to his truck, jumped in, and hit the starter. The diesel engine coughed once and clattered to life, and the vehicle started forward with a jerk. He hit the brakes, leaned out through the window, and tried to make like he was impatient. It didn't work. He couldn't help but grin at me.

"C'mon. Let's hit the trail." And we did.

After almost fifteen minutes of slow, bone-jarring, back-twisting, knee-cracking agony, the road widened a little and the big green truck finally came to halt, much to everyone's relief. I got out of my Maxima and walked around it. The shiny black surface was a vast map of tiny scratches made by its passage through the overhanging branches.

"I told ya," Evans said as he joined me and surveyed the damage. I wasn't too bothered; it was all superficial and most of it, I was sure, would buff out, but damn it.

"So where are we?" I asked.

"About a quarter mile off Haley Road. That was the main road... yeah, yeah, I know. Some main road, huh? Well, this is a forest, damn it. Anyway, the site is about a hundred yards that way." He pointed down the trail over the hood of his truck.

It was a pleasant woodland trail, ideal for hiking, although how the hell anyone would find it I had no idea. These were the game fields. Be that as it may, it was a beautiful winter's day. The sun was shining through the trees—some bare, some conifers—casting beams of light and shade that gave the place an ethereal, cathedral-like ambiance. Beautiful.

I grabbed Jacque's bag out of the trunk, asked her to take my Benelli and the camera, and I set off down the trail toward the site, photographs in hand, walking slowly, most of the time with my eyes closed.

I can feel it.

No, I don't believe in ghosts, but sometimes I get this feeling.... I can't describe it. It's just a feeling. And every once in a while....

I walked slowly, stopping every few yards, opening my eyes, gazing down the trail, closing them and moving on again. Finally, the track widened slightly, but even then it was little more than a couple of wheel ruts in the overgrown grass.

This is it.

And it was. Just a few yards ahead and to the left was the stump of a hornbeam tree, easily recognizable by its fluted trunk. I checked the photographs. *That's the one.*

It was maybe three feet in diameter and had been cut high enough to form a stool or seat. It was old, weathered, though more so on the southwest side. All of its bark was long gone.

I stopped, dropped the bag, took the camera from Jacque, and began to photograph the area. Why, after all these years? To compare the site as I saw it today with the photos I still had in my hand. I wanted to see how much the area had changed. I photographed the stump from every angle. I walked on down the trail a few yards, then back again, trying to get a feel for what it must have been like that day back in 2002.

Not too different, I think.

I returned to the stump, looked at the photographs, stared some more, looked around at the track and the trees. Except for the stump, it was an unremarkable spot in the forest.

So why here? He's finished for the day. He's walking back to his vehicle, to meet his friends. He has his gun either over his shoulder, or under his arm....

"Hand me the gun please, Jacque." She did.

I took it from her and handed her the photos and the camera, and then walked a few yards back down the trail. I turned and laid the Benelli over my right shoulder, the butt of the gun facing back down the trail. *No, that's not it. Not comfortable. He was done shooting for the day so, if what she said was right....*

This time I broke the action of the gun, and replaced it, still holding the tips of the barrels, the butt facing back down the trail. *Better, but if he tripped and fell there's no way he could have fallen on it and shot himself with the breach open.*

I removed the gun from my shoulder and cradled it in the crook of my right arm, still open at the breach, muzzles facing toward the stump. *Even better, but the same goes. If he tripped and fell, the gun would have hit the ground muzzles first and he couldn't have shot himself.*

I closed the breach and again cradled the gun in the crook of my right arm.

Nope. If he'd tripped, the muzzles of the gun would have dug into the dirt, and they didn't. So how the hell could he have shot himself? He could have sat on the stump, I suppose, put the muzzle against his chest, and used a stick to push the trigger, but... nah! The blast would have blown him backward off the stump. He would have been on his back, right about... there. Hmmmm. But he was on his face, over there.

I laid the Benelli against the stump and took the photos from Jacque again, sorted through them, found the two I was looking for—the spot where the body had been: the stump and the spot on the trail—and handed the rest back. I glanced at the Benelli leaning against the stump, and then a light went on in my head. *Suppose.... Just suppose he stopped here for a moment, sat down to take a rest, maybe even take a leak. He would have laid the gun down against the stump just like I did. In which case....*

"How long ago was that tree culled, John, do you know?"

"Long before I joined the TWRA. Twenty, twenty-five years ago, I suppose?"

I looked at the photos. The stump had been much the same then as it was now. The bark was gone even then, and there was green algae on the north side spreading west, bare gray wood to the south and east.

Photos in hand, I walked to the spot where the body had been found. It was maybe eight or ten feet east of the stump. I looked at it, then at my feet, and I shook my head.

"Something's not right," I said, more to myself than to the others. "No matter how he was carrying the gun, he couldn't have fallen on it and shot himself and, lying how and where he is the photos, he couldn't have committed suicide either. You say, Mrs. Nicholson, that he would have been carrying the gun with the breach open, but the photos clearly show it was closed. Now watch this."

I grabbed the Benelli, took a plastic evidence bag from my jacket pocket, and covered the muzzles with it. The gun went under my arm, breach closed, and I walked along the trail at a fast pace. I pretended to stumble forward. As I did, the muzzles of the gun tilted straight down toward the dirt—and would have dug deep into it if I hadn't pulled back. I looked at the others.

"So, you see. Even if he *was* carrying it with the breach closed and he tripped.... Well, now you know. The only way he could have shot himself would have been to sit on the stump, place the barrels against his chest, and push the trigger with a stick, and he could indeed have done that, but he didn't. We know that because he was found here, on the trail. Not over there." I set the Benelli down again, leaning it against the stump as before, with the trigger guard facing up, and stood back, stared at it, nodded.

I took two steps back, then turned and looked at the spot where the body had been. The others stared at me expectantly. I grinned.

"Let's think for a minute," I said. "We know he'd shot his limit. We know it was the end of the day. We can imagine that he must have been tired. We can also imagine he might have needed the bathroom. So he lays his gun against the stump, like so—maybe he even lays his bird on top of the stump—and he does what he needs to do, and is about to pick up his gun and prize when someone comes. One of the other three, maybe, or all of them; who knows?

"So he's standing somewhere here, close to the stump. The other person shoots him, poses the body, undoes his bootlace, picks up the gun and positions it under the body. Then he hides in the trees and waits for the others. He joins them and one of them calls for help...." I paused, took out my iPhone, and checked the signal—two bars, enough. "Does that make sense?"

Helen Nicholson was already nodding. So was Jacque, but Evans was looking at me skeptically.

"Come on, Harry. That's a hell of a stretch."

"Okay. So you tell me how the hell he could have

fallen on the gun, however he might have been carrying it, and shot himself."

He didn't answer.

"Okay. I understand; it's a stretch. Let's try something else then."

I opened the backpack, took out the luminol, the black light, and tarp, and laid them out on the ground, and then I heard Evans laughing. I looked up at him quizzically.

"You gotta be kidding, Harry. After all these years you expect to find blood?"

"Not on the trail, but maybe, just maybe, we might find some here." I pointed to the stump.

He shook his head. "No friggin' way."

"You're probably right, but let's see shall we? Can't hurt to try."

First, I sprayed the luminol on the east and south sides of the stump, then I draped the tarp over the muzzle of the Benelli, creating a makeshift dark tent, and then I crawled inside with the black light. "*Yes!*" I all but shouted. "John. C'mere."

He came.

"Look!"

He stared in wonder at the faint glow of what appeared to be high-velocity impact blood spatter. And yes, it was faint, but it was definitely there, just where the flutes of the trunk had protected it from the weather, although the years had obviously taken their toll.

"Damn it, Harry. I don't believe it. How the hell did you know?"

"I didn't. I was hoping. But look, even back in the office, when I first saw the photos, I had my doubts that he could have shot himself. Now I know for damned sure he didn't."

We backed out from under the tent.

"Jacque, get the camera set up and let's photograph the spatter."

She did, and went to work.

"Mrs. Nicholson," I said, "you were right. Your son was murdered, but whether or not I can figure out who killed him... well, I'll try. You can count on it."

She was crying. She turned away and walked back down the trail to my car, her shoulders hunched forward, hands to her face.

I waited until Jacque had finished taking the photos. "You sure we got them?" I asked her. The look she gave me would have withered an oak tree. I grinned at her. "Okay. I need to do one more thing. C'mon, John, I need you to observe this please."

We crawled back under the tent together. I shone the black light and, picking the very best spots, I carved several large chips out of the tree with my pocketknife—not an easy job, considering the hardness of the wood. Evans watched as I put the chunks of wood into an evidence bag, sealed it, signed it, then handed it to him to witness, which he did, and then I tucked it safely away in the inside pocket of my jacket.

Back in the sunlight, I pulled off the tarp, folded it, stuffed it back into the bag along with the black light and the luminol, and went to pick up the Benelli.... I'd laid it down against the stump while I folded the tarp, and then I paused, and I looked at the gun, and then at the spot where Peter Nicholson died, and I smiled.

Nah. I couldn't get that lucky... could I? Maybe I could!

We strolled back to the vehicles where Helen was sitting, eyes red and still wet, in the backseat of the Maxima. I told John Evans thanks, and that I'd be in touch, and he left; two minutes later, with the Benelli and the equipment safely in the trunk and the precious wood chips still in my inside pocket—I knew, because I'd checked at least five times—we followed him out.

7

TUESDAY, JANUARY 10, 2:00 P.M

The first thing I did when we returned to my offices was send Helen Nicholson on her way. I didn't want her involved in the investigation if she didn't have to be. I had a feeling it was about to get nasty, and I'm rarely wrong about such things. Then, after I made coffee, I went to get Peter Nicholson's Browning shotgun from the gun room, a walk-in safe in the back office. Next, I gathered together everyone I figured might at some stage be concerned with what I was about to do and I had them join me in the conference room: Jacque, Tim, Ronnie Hall—Peter Nicholson had been a financier of sorts—and Bob and Heather.

I placed the evidence bag with the gun inside it on the table, my own little baggie with the wood chips next to it, and the box of evidence along with the bag full of Nicholson's clothing in the middle of the table. While I waited for everyone, I sorted through the contents of the box again.

There were the files I'd glanced through earlier that morning, and I set those aside in favor of what looked like a fairly comprehensive forensics report on the gun and the contents of the smaller box—shotgun shells, shotgun pellets, the clothing and boots... but.... There was nothing to indicate what had happened to the clothing and guns that belonged to the other three men.

*Strange. They must have checked all that stuff, especially the weapons. What the hell happened to it? Why is there no mention of it here? I need to talk to—*I looked at my notes—*Sergeant Ron Fowler, Retired. Surely to God they did.*

It took a few minutes for everyone to get their coffee, iPads, notebooks, recorders, whatever, and be ready to go so, while they rustled around, I picked up one of the 8mm video tapes and looked at the baggie label.

Interview Mr. Heath Myers. Friday, May 3, 2002. Present: Lt. Wade Brewer, Hamilton County Sheriff's Dept. & Sgt. Ronald Fowler. Timed in at 6:17 p.m. Timed out at 6:48 p.m.

I DROPPED it back in the box. *Thirty-one minutes. What kind of an interview is that?* I picked up several more. They were all much the same, but three were labeled: *Scene of Accident, blah, blah, blah.* And a fourth was a record of the autopsy timed at fifty-eight minutes.

I looked around the table. Everybody was seated and looking at me expectantly.

"Bob, Heather, I brought you in on this so you'll know what's going on, and in case I need you later. Tim, you know why you're here. Ronnie, I have a feeling you're going to be up to your neck in this before we know it, so pay close attention. Jacque, you'll be working with me for a couple of days. Leslie and Margo will have to cover for you. Will that work?"

"Oh, yes. That will work just fine."

"Good, then let's get on with it."

I started by bringing them up to speed on what had occurred prior to the visit to Prentice Cooper: Helen Nicholson's visit and the circumstances of her son's death. I finished with a brief rundown of our visit to the scene and what we'd discovered there. Then I got started.

"So this is what we have: We now know for sure that it would have been impossible for Nicholson to have fallen on his gun and shot himself, and yet the autopsy report states that he died from a contact wound. Looking at the weapon through the plastic, there does indeed seem to be blood on the barrels of the weapon, but it doesn't look like blowback, which is what I'd expect to see from a contact shot. What I do see is blood smeared on the ends of the barrels." I laid my hand on the evidence bag, and continued.

"We also know from the way the body was found—its position on the trail, and the position of the gun—that he didn't commit suicide either, so that leaves only homicide. Any questions so far?" I looked at them each in turn. Nothing. I nodded, and continued.

"So, that raises questions. Namely, how exactly *did* he die? Who killed him, and why? We're looking for motive, means, and opportunity, and we seem to have plenty enough of each to go around." I paused and removed three 8 × 10 photographs from the box.

"Nicholson, the victim, was on a turkey hunt in Prentice Cooper State Forest with three friends—or two friends and one murderer." I pinned the three photos side by side on the corkboard.

"Ellis Warren," I said as I pinned up the first photo, "now Circuit Court Judge Warren..."

"Oh shit," Bob muttered.

"...Alex Harrison, now Acting United States Attorney Harrison..."

"Oh jeez." This time it was Heather.

I nodded and pinned up the final photo. "...and Heath Myers. Now managing partner of Myers, Occum & Pearson, Attorneys at Law or, as the Three Stooges would call them, Dewey, Screwum, and Howe; Myers, A.K.A. Dewey, is a longtime competitor of my father's. August will not be pleased to know who I'm up against, I think."

I looked at my crew. "Yes, I know who and what they are. I also know, or at least I'm pretty damn sure, that one of these three men murdered Peter Nicholson...."

"How do we know that?" Jacque asked. "They were there. That much we know, but couldn't some other hunters have been there too? It was, after all, hunting season."

I nodded. "It's possible. Anything's possible, but I doubt it. Hunting permits are allocated by lottery in designated areas. These four would have had that location pretty much to themselves." I paused and turned and stared at the three photographs, and as I did so I had that God-awful feeling that someone had just pissed on my grave.

"Harrison is a nasty piece of work, a damned pit-bull," I said. "He's also a winner, and doesn't care how he wins. I'm not saying he's crooked, although Amanda says all three of them are, but I do know he'll bend the law almost to the breaking point to get what he needs. He'll lie and cheat and he's fearless, tough, and arrogant."

I looked again at the three photos.

"Myers is a little different He's a slick corporate lawyer, cunning," I said. "He's smart; he knows the law better than almost anyone I know, and he gets the job done. There are more frauds on disability because of him than there are legitimate cases.

"Warren is... tough, merciless, arrogant, and often biased. Back in the day, he would have given Judge Parker a run for his money. I don't know if he's on the take or not, but it wouldn't surprise me if he were. I've run up against him several times; he doesn't like me and he doesn't like my father." I smiled. "And yet they play golf together. August almost always beats him. The score, I think, is something like eighteen to three, and Judge Warren hates to lose... at anything, which is why he keeps coming back for more." I stared up at his photograph. *He's one competitive SOB, and he's not going to take my interference well. There's going to be trouble, that's for sure.*

"Okay. So here's how we'll do it. Jacque and I will go over the forensics and incident reports. Ronnie, I want full financial histories on all four men. I want to know exactly what financial business Peter Nicholson was in when he died, and I want to know who benefitted from his death. We need motives, people, motives. Tim, you should have backgrounds for me."

He grinned, shoved his glasses up the bridge of his nose with his forefinger, nodded, and placed a pile of neatly stapled reports in front of me.

"Four men, five sets of each, just as you ordered; I also made an extra copy for myself."

"Anything stand out?"

"Yes, in fact, I—"

"Good, but not right now, Tim," I interrupted him. "I have too much to get through first. Later, okay?"

He looked a little crushed, but nodded.

"Now, let's talk about the original investigation. As far as I can see, there wasn't one. There was a cover up.

"Going by what little information there is in the incident report, the medical examiner arrived on site at around 4:55, did a quick walk around the body, declared it an accident, and left. He was there less than ten minutes. An autopsy was ordered—routine in such cases—and that also seems to have been quick and superficial. Verdict: accidental death; the injury that killed him is described as a contact wound from a 12-gauge shotgun."

I picked up Nicholson's Browning and peered through the plastic window of the bag. As I'd mentioned earlier, there were brown smears on the left side of the two barrels at the muzzles that extended down the barrels for perhaps three to three and a half inches.

Bullshit! I don't believe it. I'll get this sucker re-examined.

"I also have reason to believe that there may be high-velocity impact blood spatter on the right side of this weapon, but I'll have to get Mike Willis to confirm that." I placed the gun back on the table.

"Okay. Nicholson has been dead a long time, so there's no great rush; the first forty-eight expired more than fourteen years ago, so we have all the time in the world to get it right; we'll do it step by step.

"Jacque, you and I will be interviewing these three people." I waved a hand in the direction of the photos on the corkboard. "It won't be easy. They may refuse to talk to us. We'll also be interviewing the investigating officer, the sheriff at the time—yeah, maybe even Israel Hands. He's in the Atlanta Federal Penitentiary. And the medical examiner—" I looked at my notes "—Doctor Carl Bowden. And Jacque, don't be afraid to jump in and ask questions, of them or me. If you think of something, ask it. Are you good with all this?" *What a stupid question; she's been waiting for this moment all of her life.*

"Yeah, boss!"

"One more thing, Jacque: go get my old M&P9 from

the gun room. From now on it never leaves your side, and I want you to go get some time in on the range, this evening, yes?"

"Um," Bob said hesitantly, "you going to fill Kate in on all of this?"

"Not right now, no. She's city. All of this took place in the county, so it's out of her jurisdiction; and it's almost as old as she is." *An exaggeration, but you get the idea.* "That's why I brought Jacque into it.... Oh, sh... I'm sorry, Jacque. That didn't come out right. I would have brought you in anyway; you earned it—time on the job, loyalty, attention to detail, competence...." I hesitated. "And you saved my damned life that day up on the mountain. There's no one I'd rather have backing me up than you."

She looked mollified, but said nothing.

"Heather. How busy are you right now?"

"Not too bad; nothing urgent. You need me to do something?"

"Yeah," I said. "Warren married Nicholson's widow less than two years after he died. I want to know if they were having an affair at the time of his death. If they were, we have motive. I need you to look into that for me, please."

"Okay. I'll get right on it."

"So... Jacque. Interviews. We'll start with what's left of the investigating officers, and unfortunately that's just Ron Fowler. I want to hear the story from him before I decide what to do next, but sometime over the next few days we'll need to go through the post report with Doc

Sheddon…. I'm not even sure if Carl Bowden is still alive. I do know he retired years ago."

"He is," Heather said. "He's at the Meadowlands Nursing Home on East Brainerd."

I frowned. "How the hell do you know that?"

"I saw him there last week. I was visiting my mother."

That was a first. Heather did not talk about her private life, *ever*.

"He was in a wheelchair, in the common room. Looked spaced out to me. Just sort of staring out of the window at the ducks on the pond."

"Okay, well, I want to know why he declared it an accident. So we'll need to see him too. We'll do that right after we see Fowler. Then we'll figure out what to do next. Okay, that's it for now. Back to work, people. But Jacque, Tim, you stay here. Ronnie, have you got what you need?"

He did.

But I did not. I needed caffeine. "I'm making more coffee—anyone else…." And it was right then that I realized I hadn't called Amanda. I looked at my watch. It was almost three thirty.

"Sorry guys," I said. "Go get your own coffee. I need to make a call. I'll buzz you when I'm done."

I waited until I was alone and then hit the speed dial. She answered on the second ring.

"Ah," she said. "So you are still alive. I was beginning to wonder." She was joking. I could tell. At least I thought I could.

"Yeah... I'm sorry. I just got carried away is all. I have a case."

"I know you do. You told me, remember? So, when?"

"No later than six o'clock. I promise. What's for dinner?"

"Jesus, Harry. You've got nerve. We've been home ten minutes and I'm supposed to turn into this sweet little housewife? I don't think so. You have two options: pick something up on the way home, or take me out. Which is it going to be?"

I sighed. "Meet me at the Public House at six. That okay?"

I could almost hear her smile. "That would be nice, but not the Public House. No. First, we were there only yesterday for lunch, second, I don't want to drive, and third, it will be too busy; I want to be alone with you. How about—"

"How about I come home, change, and we go to Ruth's Chris? I'll book a table for eight o'clock. Will that work?"

"It will. Don't be late. I love you." And she disconnected.

I went to the outer office, beckoned for Margo, and asked her to make the reservation for me. I also asked her to make sure we got a quiet table, and to let me know when she'd confirmed. Then I grabbed a cup of joe and headed back to the conference room. Jacque was seated at the table sipping her coffee. Tim didn't have any, thank God.

I've mentioned Tim before, but you should know he's

a geek in every sense of the word. Dropped out of Georgia Tech as a seventeen-year-old sophomore and has been hacking since his dad bought him his first IBM PC back in 1998. He never got caught although, reading between the lines, he came close a couple of times. He says he's reformed. *And if you believe that, you'd better watch out because there's a squadron of pigs overhead and they're about to offload.*

He's also the busiest member of my staff and I love him like a son. Most of the time.

"Ok, Tim," I said, as I opened my iPad and seated myself at the right side of the table, next to the corkboard. "Let's have it. What were you able to dig up?"

He picked up his set of papers, settled back in his chair, shoved his glasses up the bridge of his nose, stared down at the first page... and I waited. The boy had a bad habit of retreating into some weird world of his own; I sometimes wondered if he suffered from some form of narcolepsy.

Finally: "Tim?" I asked quietly, as I handed one of the sets to Jacque.

"Uh...." He looked up at me. "Oh, yeah. Well, if you look at the papers I made up for you, you'll see it's all pretty standard stuff. All four, now three, are brilliant men, but I found little to set them apart except for Judge Ellis Warren and Peter Nicholson. But let's do the other two first, if that's okay."

I nodded. He flipped pages, adjusted his glasses, and began.

"All four went to Baylor High School, where they

formed a strong bond; all four graduated with over 4.0 GPAs. They all went on to good schools. As far as I can tell, Myers and Harrison are squeaky clean." He looked up at me, got no reaction, then continued.

"Harrison graduated from Stanford Law and went to work for the Feds as an assistant prosecutor. Now he's the Acting US Attorney for the Eastern District of Tennessee.

"Heath Myers also went to Stanford Law, but he went into private practice here in Chattanooga. He learned the ropes at Robinson and Hart, and then opened his own law office with a couple partners in 2009. They specialize in corporate law." He smiled at me when he said that last bit, knowing as he did that my father had had several run-ins with the erstwhile Heath Myers. "He's successful, wealthy, has lots of friends, and is well respected... well, by most of his peers; some, not so much." Again he smiled at me. "Although he does have a certain reputation for cutting corners...."

"He's a damned crook, is what he is," I said. They both looked at me.

"Just saying," I said with a shrug.

"Well, as I said," Tim continued. "They both seem to be clean. Now, on to Peter Nicholson." He flipped through the pages until he found what he was looking for, then he looked up at me.

"This one is probably more Ronnie's area of expertise than mine, but I'll give you the basics, then you can bring him in if you like."

"Wait," I said. "If we need him, let's get him in here

now. No point in going over it twice."

I picked up the phone and buzzed Ronnie. He arrived a couple of minutes later and took a seat next to Jacque. I nodded for Tim to continue.

He nodded. "Peter Nicholson earned a master's degree in finance from Booth—University of Chicago—one of the top finance schools in the US. From there he went to work for Charles Schwab and eventually became a stockbroker specializing in the NASDAC...."

"When was this?" Ronnie asked with a knowing look.

Tim flipped through pages, and Ronnie waited with a sly smile on his lips.

"That would have been in... 1995...." Tim and Ronnie said "1995" in unison.

Ronnie leaned back in his chair and laced his fingers together behind his neck.

"The beginning of the dot-com bubble," he said. "I knew it. And right there, if I'm not mistaken, is your motive. They were friends, right? I betcha one or more of the other three, maybe all of them, lost a bunch of money during the collapse and blamed Nicholson for it."

Tim was right. This was exactly what I'd hired Ronnie Hall for. He's the best in the business, a financial wizard, and about as different from Tim as the proverbial chalk from cheese. He came to me when I first opened the agency and now heads up my white-collar investigations division. His background is in banking and he has a masters in finance from the London School of Economics.

"Can you find out, Ronnie?"

"Yes. It may take a little while, but it's all there if you know where to look. I'll start with their finances. Should be easy enough."

"Good. There's no real rush, but soon would be good." I turned back to Tim. "What else?"

"Let's talk about Judge Warren."

Now this should be interesting.

"I don't know about a financial motive, but in 2004 he married Nicholson's widow. That might be a motive, right? If he was having an affair with—"

"Yes, Helen Nicholson told me about that. And I think you may be right. I know the judge. He's a rare piece of work. I've thought for years that he's corrupt, but proving it... well, let's just say he's good, very good. Maybe 'bad' would be the operative word. What else?"

"Nothing I can put my finger on, just a lot of innuendo and... oh, yeah; you're not going to like this: he was, and probably still is, good buddies with Congressman Harper."

I already knew that too, and I'd had the congressman on my mind for several weeks. It started on the sailboat out in the Caribbean. I was lying out on the foredeck daydreaming when he suddenly popped into my head, and I had an allover uneasy feeling that hadn't ever really gone away. Maybe it was an omen....

Who the hell knows? I killed his daughter. He sure as hell isn't going to let that go, even if it was completely justified.

"Warren," Tim continued, "is the only child of a fairly well-to-do Chattanooga family. After high school he went on to Harvard Law, where he graduated in the top fifth percentile. As you know, he's now a circuit court judge." He paused and flipped the page. "Other than his friendship with Harper, and the public outrage when he married Mary Ann Nicholson, he's clean. He's a tough SOB, though."

"That he is," I mused, "as I well know from experience."

I kicked back in my chair, stared over at the three photographs, and thought about what I'd heard and what I knew about the people in them. Their eyes seemed to stare right back at me, mocking me, daring me.

What the hell happened that day? Which one of you.... Maybe it was all of you.

"Boss?" Jacque asked, quietly.

"Hm?"

"Nothing. I thought for a moment we'd lost you, that's all."

I nodded. "I was trying to get my head around what happened that day. Why was there no in-depth investigation? How the hell did they class it as an accident? Nothing adds up, except for the fact that we are dealing with four very influential individuals, one of whom is dead and most likely murdered by one of the other three."

I stared up at the photos some more, shook my head, and came back down to earth... well, from Prentice Cooper State Forest, where I'd been playing out, in my imagination, as many of the possible scenarios of what happened that day as I could think of. *One of them killed him. Had to. Okay. Let's go to work.*

"Ronnie," I said, leaning forward over the desk and handing him one of Tim's information packages, "I want those financials, all of them, but Warren is the one I'm most interested in, right now anyway.

"Tim, keep digging. Dig deep. Find out everything you can about Judge Warren, Mary Ann Nicholson-Warren, and Myers and Harrison. If there's any dirt on any of them, I want to know. I especially want to know if there was any gossip about Mary Ann and Warren.

"Okay, guys. Get to it."

I waited until they left, and then I turned to Jacque.

"Tomorrow you and I are going to call on Fowler and Bowden. If we can get that done by lunchtime, we'll go visit my dad and see what he knows." I grinned. "Hell, we might even run into the Warrens. That would be fun."

The look on her face was a picture. This was new territory for her, and I wasn't sure she was entirely comfortable.

"You okay?" I asked.

"I am." She smiled. "It's just... well, a bit overwhelming, you know?"

"I do," I replied, and I did, "but you'll get used to it soon. In the meantime...." I looked at my watch; it was almost five. I glanced down at the box on the table and sighed. "I need to be home by six thirty, so let's take a quick look through this stuff so we know what we're talking about tomorrow."

She nodded.

"This is all of the evidence—at least I think it is—

that's left from the original investigation. As for what the hell happened to the rest of it... well, your guess is as good as mine. The autopsy report is simple enough—too simple. The colored still photos are helpful, but before you leave if you could run prints from the Nikon we took this morning, well... I'm particularly interested in the ones of the stump and the bloodstains. These—" I picked them up and shuffled through them "—the originals are good, they cover the site in detail, and these close-ups of the wound in Nicholson's chest show plenty of detail, but..." I looked closely at them, "they're a little fuzzy, slightly out of focus...."

What? I shook my head. Something about the wound.... *I dunno, and I don't have time to try to figure it out now.*

I set those photos aside until I had more time. *Whew!*

"We need to go see Doc Sheddon too. I want him to take a look at the report and the photographs. If you would, please. Have Tim make copies of the original photos, and you make copies of the report. Okay. I've had enough for today, and I'm taking Amanda out this evening." I rose to my feet. "Give Fowler a call and see if you can set something up for first thing in the morning. Give Meadowlands a call too. See if we can get in to see Bowden, and call Doc Sheddon; we can see him whenever he's got a few minutes. If there's a problem, call me. If not...."

"I know; you'll see me in the morning."

I nodded. "You got it."

8

WEDNESDAY, JANUARY 11, 8:30 A.M

I rose early the following morning. I'd made it home the night before just in time to save myself from... well, you know. The steaks at Ruth's Chris were outstanding, as always, and we made it back home in time to watch the evening news, only we didn't. I was so tired I fell asleep on the sofa, and that's where I woke up at five that morning, cold and groggy. On any other day I would have cleared the cobwebs by going for a run, but not that day. It was raining—no, it was storming, and the view over the city.... Well, there wasn't one. Visibility was almost zero. We were up among the clouds: rain and dense fog—it was enough to kill the mood of even the most upbeat person, one of which... I ain't.

The drive down the mountain that morning was a test, not only of my driving skills on the mountain roads in the middle of a thunderstorm, but also of nerve. At 7:15 a.m. it was still dark, and the road, blanketed in fog, was a virtual river. The water cascaded down off the heights onto the road in torrents. And it was cold, barely above freezing. I had the climate control in the Maxima set to a balmy 75 degrees, but even so, I couldn't help wishing I was back on the sunny beaches of Calypso Key.

Once I was off the mountain, though, and onto Broad Street, things got a little better. Still, by the time I reached my offices I felt like I'd driven a hundred miles. Downtown was half flooded and still dark, and I braved the few yards from my car to the side door in a downpour, collar turned up, keys in hand. Fortunately, Jacque had arrived a few minutes earlier and it was already unlocked.

She was dressed in jeans, knee-high boots, and a white roll-neck sweater that contrasted starkly with her dark skin and even darker hair. The Smith and Wesson M&P9 was holstered on her right hip, something I'd never seen before, at least as far as she was concerned. It was something I was going to have to get used to.

My own Heckler and Koch VP9 was secured in its shoulder rig under my leather jacket. I too was wearing a roll-neck sweater, but mine was black, as were my jeans and jacket. I was dressed for comfort.

I usually get my own coffee—I don't expect the people who work for me to wait on me too—but today Jacque had already made it for me, and a twenty-ounce Yeti cup was waiting for me on my desk, the gas fire logs on and turned up high. For the first time that day, I felt quite comfortable.

Other than my home, my personal office is the one place where I'm truly happy. It's as comfortable as I could possibly have made it, and it cost me more to decorate than I care to reveal. It has all the trimmings: a huge, antique mahogany desk, leather chairs, iMac computer, but I also spent a lot of money on the decor. The walls are paneled with dark walnut; there are two floor-to-ceiling bookshelves; the ceiling is painted a soft shade of magnolia and home to a huge crystal chandelier, something I picked out on a whim for reasons even I can't recall. The windows are dressed with ivory sheers that contrast with heavy brocade drapes that match the carpet. Several pieces of artwork—local scenes by local artists—adorn the walls. They're not worth a fortune, but they were costly enough. There's also a small drinks cabinet where I keep my special goodies, including several bottles of Laphroaig Quarter Cask scotch whisky. But the focal point of the room is the floor-to-ceiling stone fireplace. The chimney is fake, but the gas logs provide plenty of warmth and atmosphere. The room had been designed by a master. Her intention was to impress my clients, to instill a sense opulence and success. She claimed that was important. Whatever. I like it because it's a retreat, a place to go when I need to be alone, shut out the rest of the world, and relax, either in the huge leather chair behind my desk or in front of the fire.

"So," I said, dropping into one of the chairs by the fireplace, coffee in hand, "what's the plan?"

Jacque sat down on the other side of the coffee table. "We have an appointment with Mr. Fowler at nine and the receptionist at Meadowlands said we could drop by anytime other than between noon and one thirty, which is when they serve lunch. Dr. Sheddon will not be available until tomorrow, but he said we can go by there at nine, provided nothing happens overnight."

"Hah," I said. "The way the gangs are acting up right now.... Okay, nine o'clock it is. How are Bob and the others doing out there?"

"They're fine. Everything... all of the cases are up to scratch and on schedule. Ronnie and Tim are still gathering what you need. They should have it for you later today. Other than that...."

I nodded, stared into the flames, sipped on my coffee, and was soon lost in thought, back in Prentice Cooper. I could picture what they said had happened, or what was supposed to have happened, in my mind's eye.

Hell, shotguns don't go off when you drop them. Well, rarely, but for sure not in a situation like that. Where were the others? What the hell was he doing on his own.... If he was on his own. I know....

"Harry? *Harry!*"

"Huh? What?"

"Where were you?" she asked. "I was talking to you. You didn't hear a word I said to you, did you?"

I screwed my eyes shut and shook my head. "No, Jacque, I didn't. I'm sorry. What did you say?"

"I said that it's time we got out of here. It's fifteen to nine."

WEDNESDAY, JANUARY 11, 9:00 A.M

R on Fowler lived in Hixson, in north Chattanooga, in a neat little tri-level on Cloverdale Loop. It was a drive of about eight miles from the office but, because of my reverie, the heavy rain, and the early morning traffic, we arrived some ten minutes late. Not that it mattered to Fowler; he was obviously pleased to have any visitors at all.

He must have been waiting for us, because before I could ring the bell, the front door opened and there he was, a big grin on his face and his hand stuck out for me to shake, which I did.

He was in his early sixties, fit and trim, dressed in jeans and a blue plaid flannel shirt. His face was drawn, the high cheekbones prominent, the mouth wide, the lips full. His white hair was in dire need of a trim, but it was neatly combed back over his forehead and hung almost to his collar. His eyes were brown and full of life.

I thought this guy was supposed to be in bad health.

Without waiting for me to make the introductions, he ushered us up the stairs into the living room, which was sparsely furnished but with all the necessities of life in retirement: a sixty-inch flat-screen TV, a couch, a recliner, and a coffee table. He had Jacque and I sit together on the couch, and then he went to the adjoining kitchen and returned with a tray with mugs and a full pot of steaming coffee.

He poured the coffee, offered milk and sugar, then picked up his mug, sat down in the recliner, leaned back and smiled knowingly, first at Jacque and then at me. And he waited.

"Mr. Fowler," I began, "I'm...."

"I know who you are, Harry," he interrupted me. "You're the one who put that prick Israel Hands away." He looked at Jacque. "But you. Who are you?"

"I'm Jacque Hale, Mr. Starke's personal assistant."

"Nah. You're not," he said, rising from his chair and offering her his hand. "Not packing a piece like that." Her jacket was unzipped, and he nodded at the exposed holster on her hip.

She shook his hand and smiled, "I am his PA. This is my first time out in the field, Mr. Fowler."

He nodded, his lips clamped together in a down-turned smile. "Lucky man, Harry. I know you know who I am, so please, call me Ron."

"You're very young to be retired," she said.

He seemed pleased by the compliment, nodded, and said, "I did my thirty years. Retired two years ago. Couldn't handle it any longer than that. Couldn't pass the lieutenant's exam, and... well, he'll tell you." He nodded at me. "The blood and guts of the homicide division is more than some men can handle; I'm one of them. Now I do a little security, read a lot, and watch TV. It's not a bad life. So, there you are. Now, Harry, what can I do for you? No! Don't tell me. Let me tell you. You're here about Peter Nicholson, right?"

"How did you know that?"

He shook his head, smiling. "I knew it. She'll never give up. His mother. She's become quite a friend.... Oh, she didn't tell you? Funny that, because it was me that suggested she hire you." He sipped on the huge mug of black coffee and stared at me over the rim; wisps of steam curled up in front of his eyes.

The hell you did.

"She's right, you know, his mother," he said. "It wasn't an accident, but she never was going to be able to get anyone's attention. It's going to take someone like you. The players are too highly placed. It was covered up from the minute Hands arrived on the scene. He knew. Wade knew, and I knew. Wade died praying for forgiveness. I hope he gets it. Me? I was just Wade's partner. That whole department under Israel Hands was... I want to say corrupt, but that's not true. Most of the department was honest, but Hands ran it like... like his own private army. You did good work putting him away." He looked gloomily down into his mug, obviously lost in thought, and I could sympathize. The sheriff back then had been an asshole and a crook to boot.

"You want to tell me about it?" I asked.

He looked up, startled, then said, "There's not much to tell. Nicholson, Myers, Warren, and Harrison drew a good spot on the spring turkey hunt. They arrived early that morning and took their designated spots; they were spread out across several hundred yards of forest. They met for lunch around noon, and then split up again. From time to time they heard shots, each assuming it was one of the others, or maybe even neighboring hunters. They called it a day just before four o'clock that afternoon. Myers, Warren, and Harrison were heading back to the cars when they found him. From the way he was lying on the trail, so they said, they assumed he'd had an accident, tripped and fell on his gun. Anyway, one of them called it in, Harrison, I think it was. Wade and me were first on the scene. We happened to be on Highway 27 a couple miles from the ranger station. We arrived at 4:35 along with two TWRA rangers."

"Was one of them John Evans?" I asked, more out of curiosity than a need to know.

"No. He arrived later, after they'd taken the body away. These two were... damned if I can remember their names. One was a lieutenant, the other.... Ah. Well, anyway, we made sure he was dead, then taped off the scene, took photos and video, and then waited for old man Bowden, the medical examiner. It was almost five o'clock when he arrived. Hands arrived a couple of minutes before him." He paused, thought for a moment, sipped on his coffee.

"Harry," he said, "it was the weirdest thing. Bowden, he spent less than ten minutes there, on site, and that included having the body taken to his vehicle. He walked up to the body, touched the neck to feel for a pulse, nodded, said the guy was dead, grabbed an arm and lifted the body so he could see the gun, then *dropped* it down again, walked once around it, pulled out his notebook, scribbled a couple of lines, then said, 'Accident. He tripped over his bootlace and fell on the gun. You can move the body to my car. Do it now, please.' Wade started to say something, but Hands interrupted him. He said something to the effect that the ME said it was an accident and to do as he asked and clean up while they removed the body. So we did. Harry, they couldn't get him out of there quick enough."

"Where were the other three while all this was going on?" I asked.

"Warren and company? They were at the trailhead, waiting by their cars."

"Did you talk to them?"

"I didn't. Well, I was there, but Wade did the interviews. They were short and sweet. Those guys had it together, and they had their stories down pat, almost like they'd rehearsed them. They reeled them off and when Wade tried to question them, they either repeated what they'd already said, or they just clammed up. Finally, Wade just gave up and let 'em go."

"So give me your thoughts, Ron." I said. "What do you think really happened that day?"

"You've seen the photos, right?"

I nodded. "We have them with us." Jacque handed me the file. I removed several of the photos and laid them on the coffee table. He leaned forward, adjusted them with his forefinger, stared at them.

"See, to me and Wade, the whole thing looked staged. Wade said so at the time to Sheriff Hands, but he said, and I'm paraphrasing, 'Bullshit. The ME said it was an accident, and it was. Don't try to make more of it than there is. Get rid of the goddamn perimeter tape and get down to the office and do the interviews, and then close the book on it.' And that's basically what we did."

"You said it looked staged," Jacque said. "In what way?"

"Look at the photos. How the hell did the gun end up where it is? Think about it. You trip and fall and the gun hits the dirt and flies out of your hand, right? But look at it. It's tucked nicely under him, the muzzle right at the wound. I didn't believe it then, and I don't believe it now. Look at this one." It was a close up of the right boot. "The lace is undone, spread out. That's what the they said he tripped on. He could have, but look at the boot itself."

"I don't need to," I said. "It's still tight. If he'd been walking with the lace undone it would have been loose."

"But there's more," he said.

"There is," I said. "Jacque, look at this one. Do you see anything out of the ordinary?"

She shook her head. "No, I... don't see anything. What is it?"

I looked at Fowler. "You want to tell her or shall I?"

He grinned. "Why don't you tell her?"

"Are you testing me, Ron?" I smiled at him, and he laughed.

"Maybe."

"The cuffs of his pants have been pulled up almost to his mid-calf. That happens when you sit or kneel down...."

"So," she interrupted excitedly, "he was either sitting or kneeling, which means he didn't fall... and that means someone else shot him. He was; he was murdered. Maybe not. Maybe he did it himself.... No! Not dat." There was that Jamaican accent again. "He could not have shot his own self and then arranged.... But who could have done it?

"That, my dear, is what we're trying to figure out. Ron? Any ideas?"

He slowly shook his head. "Not really, but my best guess would be Warren. He married Nicholson's widow.... And then there's the money."

"Money?" I asked. "What money?"

"Well, he was insured: two policies. One for half a million, the other for 750K. She was the sole beneficiary."

I hadn't known that but, thinking about it, it made no difference, except maybe to Warren when he married her; the others? Maybe they benefited some other way from his death, but not from the policies. Ron was right; for now, Judge Ellis Warren was the prime suspect.

"How about forensics?" I asked.

"We took the gun and his clothes, and what was in his pockets and so forth. There was nothing else. There was no forensic examination of anything. It was an accident, right?" he said was a certain amount of sarcasm. "We combed the site, but...."

"What about the other three? Did you get their clothing, guns...?"

"No. Wade wanted to, but they kicked up a fuss and Hands said there was no need since it had been ruled an accident.

"And the interviews were a goddamn joke. Warren kicked up a fuss, but he allowed us to take them only for the record. Might as well have handed them multiple choice questionnaires for all the good they were."

He leaned forward, his mug cradled in both hands, his elbows resting on his knees. He stared, unseeing, at a framed photograph on the coffee table, then he looked up at me and shook his head.

"I'd tell you good luck," he said, "but you're gonna need more than that. It's been cold, what, fifteen years? And you ain't gonna get *near* those three, let alone get 'em to talk to you, I don't care *who* you are. Call me, or come back if you need to, but...." He placed his mug on the table, leaned back in his chair, and shrugged.

We talked for a few more minutes. I asked several more questions that I really didn't get any good answers to; hell, I knew there was nothing more he could tell us. I asked only because I wanted to make sure I'd covered all the bases, and then we left.

He stood at the open front door and watched as we ran through the rain to the car. I had the feeling he didn't want us to leave, poor guy. He was still watching as we drove away.

10

WEDNESDAY, JANUARY 11, 11:00 A.M

Meadowlands Nursing Home was one of those decaying, rundown facilities you find in every town: a one-story, one-time hospital that should have been torn down and replaced years ago. The place seemed to be well run: quiet, clean, and tidy, but it was an old building that no amount of paint and new linoleum could drag into the twenty-first century.

The nurse at the reception desk looked as tired and overworked as the building, but she greeted us brightly enough.

"I'd like to see Dr. Carl Bowden, please. I have one or two questions about an old case of his...."

She shook her head. "You can see him, but it won't do you any good. He's in the advanced stages of Alzheimer's. He doesn't remember much about anything." She paused. "You still want to try?"

"I do. Please."

"Okay. Follow me."

She led us along a corridor and into a large open space, the south side of which was a single picture window with a couple of small tables and several mismatched chairs set close to them. There was also a wheelchair set facing the window; its occupant was staring out of it, seemingly into space.

She led us across the room and placed a hand gently on the old man's shoulder.

"Carl?"

He didn't move.

She leaned and whispered in his ear, "Carl?"

He started, looked up at her, and smiled. "It's beautiful," he said.

"What is, Carl?"

He nodded as he looked out of the window. "The lake. The birds. Beautiful." It was.

She looked at me, her eyes wide, astonished. "He's lucid; first time in a week. You have five minutes. Make the most of it." And she left to take a seat at one of the tables a few feet away.

"Dr. Bowden?" I said. "I'd like to talk to you. Will that be okay?"

He looked up at me and smiled. Then he looked at Jacque and his eyes lit up.

"Sit down, sit down. What did you say your names were?"

We pulled up two chairs and sat down beside him.

"My name's Harry Starke, Dr. Bowden, and this is my friend, Jacque."

He nodded, looked out of the window. "It's beautiful, isn't it?" He paused, then: "What do you want?"

There was no point in trying to make conversation. I jumped right in. "Do you remember the Peter Nicholson case, Dr. Bowden?"

He shut his eyes, screwed up his mouth, seemed to concentrate, then opened his eyes and smiled.

"The Nicholson boy. Yes. He fell on his gun. Shot himself. I remember. Caused quite a stir at the time.... Shot himself.... Tripped.... Fell on his gun. Silly man.... Beautiful. Ducks. Sometimes there are hawks."

"Dr. Bowden. You said it was an accident. Why?"

"Accident? What accident? What.... Oh, the Nicholson thing.... Because it was; you could see that it was. I was there, you know. I saw him. He was lying on the gun. Besides... besides... one of them... ah, ah, I don't remember which one: one of them said he tripped on his bootlace and fell.... Look, look at that one, the pretty colored one. It's an orgasm duck, you know."

"What?" I looked at Jacque.

"Merganza. He means a merganza duck," she whispered.

"Oh," I smiled. "Yes, that's right, Dr. Bowden, but who said it was an accident? It's not in any of the reports."

"Accident? What accident?"

Oh shit. How am I going to do this?

"The Nicholson case, Dr. You said he fell and shot himself."

"Oh... that. I... I... I don't remember. It was so long

ago. He... he said he tripped, fell on the gun. It went off; an accident. You... you could see it, the way he was lying there, on the gun.... It was all so long ago...." He paused, stared out of the window.

Jeez.

"Dr. Bowden!"

He came back with a start. "What.... Oh, it's you. What do you want?"

I looked at Jacque. She shook her head.

"Dr. Bowden," I said, quietly. "The man who told you it was an accident. I need to know who that was. Please. Concentrate. Who told you it was an accident?"

"Accident? What accident? What are you talking about? I haven't had an accident." He leaned forward in the wheelchair, put his hands on the arms as if he were about to try to stand, looked around the room, and whispered, "Where's Lily? Where is she?"

"Lily?" I asked. "Who's Lily?"

The nurse must have heard him, because she came quickly to his side. "Lily will be here soon, Carl. I'll bring her to you when she arrives." He smiled up at her and nodded, then turned again to look out of the window.

She turned to me. I stood up and she took me by the elbow, and tried to steer me toward the door. "I think it's time you left. He can't help you."

"But I have to know," I said.

She shook her head. "But he *doesn't* know. He doesn't even know Lily, his wife, has been dead for more than five years. He doesn't know who I am either, most days. Please, leave him in peace." And I did.

Outside in the parking lot, I stood for a moment, hands in my jacket pockets, and stared up at the remnants of the storm that was now, for the most part, giving the population of the mountains of Western North Carolina the benefit of its still mounting rage.

Wow. The man's a.... No, he's not. He's sick—dying, God bless him. Now what?

"You want some lunch?" I asked Jacque quietly, without taking my eyes off the low-lying clouds. "I need to go to the club and talk to my father. You can come with me or I can drop you back at the office."

She nodded. "The office, if you don't mind. There are a couple of things I need to handle. Shouldn't take more than an hour. Then I'm all yours. That okay?"

It was, and we climbed into the car and headed back. I wasn't feeling so good. Depressed by what I'd seen of a once-vibrant human being in the final throes of a terrible and debilitating disease. In fact, I wasn't in the mood for the club either, or my father, so the office was just fine for me too.

11

WEDNESDAY, JANUARY 11, 1:00 P.M

The office was deserted; everyone else had gone to lunch. Jacque went quickly about whatever it was she needed to do, and I made coffee and went to my inner sanctum to sit in front of the fire, perchance to dream.

Nah. That's not it. I'm missing the tropical sunshine, sand, sea, and rum punches... Amanda... and the Lady May. *I wonder if he'd like to sell her.... Forget it, Harry. She'd just sit there at the dock, waiting, and you'd never get there. It's a nice thought, but... maybe one day. For now, there are things you need to do.*

I got up out of the easy chair and went to my desk. Cup in hand, I stared down at the tiny collection of... *What? A few sheets of paper, a dozen or so photographs, videotapes, odds and ends of... nothing.*

"Hey!"

I hadn't heard the door open. I looked around to find Amanda standing in the doorway, smiling at me. What a sight for sore eyes. She was the woman of my dreams and I still couldn't get used to idea that she was now my wife. We'd gotten back from our honeymoon less than a week ago. *And those were six of the happiest damned weeks of my life.*

She looked gorgeous; no, she *was* gorgeous. It wasn't so much what she was wearing—jeans, boots, and a pale blue parka jacket—it was.... *Hell, she's my wife. How else should I feel?*

"Hey," I said. "What brings you here? You want coffee?"

"No, no coffee. I've had more than I need. I just dropped in to see how you were coping. Are you getting back into the swing of things?"

I nodded. "Yeah. Jacque and I've been out doing interviews. Just like old times... only different."

"Different? How?"

I shook my head, stared down at the crap on my desk. "Dunno. Just different. No sense of urgency, no... aw hell, I don't know." I looked at my watch. It was almost one in the afternoon. "Too early for a drink, I suppose?"

"Are you kidding me? Of course it is. What's wrong, Harry?"

I heaved a sigh, shook my head. "I guess I let my interview with Dr. Bowden get to me. He was in a sorry state, Amanda.... He has Alzheimer's and I couldn't help thinking, what if...."

"What if it happened to you?" she asked.

"No. That wasn't it." I looked her in the eyes, her beautiful jade green eyes, so full of life and energy, and I remembered the dull, lifeless orbs that had gazed almost unseeingly back at me less than an hour ago. "I couldn't help thinking, what if it happened to you?"

I thought she was going to laugh, but she didn't. Instead she took a step forward, put her arms around my neck, and whispered in my ear.

"That's not going to happen. Now snap out of it." She leaned back, smiled at me, kissed me gently, and said, "So tell me all about it. What have you learned?"

It was then that the door opened and Jacque stepped in. "Oh," she said, "I'm sorry. I'll come back."

"No, it's okay. Come on in. We were just catching up on... well, you know."

"I could see. How are you, Amanda? You getting used to being married to this lunk?"

"I didn't have to get used to it. I already was. We just made it official is all.... But I love it, and I'm doing well. Thank you."

"Okay," I said. "That's enough. We have work to do. At least, Jacque and I do. What are you doing the rest of the day?" I asked Amanda.

"Well, I was hoping to run through what I'd found at the station with you, but if you're busy...."

"No, not busy. Just frustrated. So let's get started." I took my seat behind my desk; Amanda and Jacque took the two guest chairs in front. "What do you have, Amanda?"

"Well, I did as you asked. I went through the archives. On the accident, there's very little, just thirty seconds or so of stock footage of the forest, a short report from a young reporter, Jennifer Lock, about the accident —she's long gone, by the way. There's ten seconds with a TWRA officer named Webb who extolled the virtues of gun safety, and a twenty-five-second interview with Heath Myers. None of it's going to be much help I'm afraid. But I put it all on a thumb drive if you want to take a look."

She handed me the drive and I opened the file on my laptop, turned it so we could all see the screen, and hit play. She was right. There wasn't much. Most of it was standard six-o'clock-news stuff. What *did* interest me was the interview with Heath Myers.

I have a master's degree in forensic psychology, and I pride myself on my ability to read people, so I paid special attention to that short piece of footage. In fact, I ran it half a dozen times.

"We don't know what happened," Myers said. "I was heading back to the car when I found him, Peter; he was down, lying on his gun. I called for help and Alex and Ellis came running. Ellis checked his pulse; Peter was dead. His bootlace was undone. We figured he'd tripped on it and fell and... I guess his gun went off. It's... it was such a shock, terrible. He was a good friend."

He looked devastated: shoulders slumped, his face pale, eyes cast down, his right hand by his side, shaking slightly. I couldn't see his other hand. If he was acting or not, I couldn't tell. If he was, he was good. Very good.

"What do you think?" I asked them.

"He seems to be... devastated," Amanda said.

"Jacque?" I asked.

"I don't know. It seemed like he was unable to look at the camera... but yes; he looks... like he's in shock?"

"Most people are camera shy when it's their first time," Amanda said, staring at the screen as I reran the interview. "Maybe it is just nerves, that and what had happened. I don't see anything unusual."

I nodded, ran it again, shook my head. "Jeez, I wish we had more. We need to look at the interview tapes. I'll get Tim on it." I picked up the phone and punched in Tim's extension.

"Hey, Tim. You got a minute?" He had. He'd just gotten back from lunch.

"Tim," I said as he came in, before he had a chance to say anything, "you know about this stuff, right?" I waved my hand at the baggie of 8mm cartridges

"Sure. Looks like Hi 8mm video, old stuff. What do you need? You need them digitized?"

I picked up the plastic bag and handed it to him. "I'd rather view them now. How can I do that? "

"You can't. Not without converting them to digital. Well, you can; you can view them on the camera that made them, or one like it, but the screen is so small it would be practically useless." He pushed his glasses higher on the bridge of his nose, and turned the bag over in his hands. "These are Sony Handycam Hi8 tapes. We have a couple of those cameras in the store room. There was a time when you could play these cartridges on a regular VCR. You had to use a special cassette, but I haven't seen one of those in years. I can convert them to digital and put them onto DVDs, and then you can view them on your computer. It'll take a while, though?"

"Oh, okay. Go ahead. Soon as you can. I need them yesterday."

"You got it. I'll have some of them done tonight. The rest, sometime tomorrow morning."

"Do the one with the interviews of Warren, Myers, and Harrison first. We'll go through them first thing."

I waited until he'd closed the door.

I picked up my little baggie of wood chips. "Jacque, I need to know whose blood is on these chips. I'm betting it's Peter Nicholson's but we don't have his DNA to make a comparison. We'll need a swab from his mother. If you would, please, give her a call and ask her to come in. Tell her I'll buy her lunch, either tomorrow or Friday. Whichever suits her best. Then get these chips off to DDC; Lindsey Oats owes me a favor so we'll get a quick turn-around, I hope."

She made a note on her iPad, and I continued, "We have an appointment with Doc Sheddon at nine tomorrow, but I'd also like for you to set up interviews with Huey, Dewey, and Louie. I want to see them tomorrow too, if possible, after we're done with Doc."

"With who?"

I grinned at her. "You know who. Warren and company."

She made more notes. "Got it. Anything else?"

"Not right now, but if I think of anything...."

She nodded and rose to her feet. "Then I'll leave you two alone and go get on with it."

"I want to talk to August," I said to Amanda as Jacque closed the door behind her. "You up for dinner at the club?" She was.

"Do you know these three?" I asked her, nodding at the board.

She thought for a moment, then said, "I know who they are, and I've met Harrison a couple of times for work interviews, but Myers and Warren I've never met."

"What did you think of Harrison?"

"Not much. He's not liked, that I do know. He also has a thing for the ladies. I can personally attest to that. He came onto me both times I met him. He's charming, in a way, but I found him a little slimy, and condescending. Other than that, he's businesslike, loves the sound of his own voice, good in the courtroom, but I've seen better. My overall impression was that he's not quite the over-achiever that he would have everyone believe... and, I don't know why, but I have a strong feeling he's less than honest. How about you? Do you know him?"

I couldn't help but smile at her. I shook my head and laughed, "Damn it, Amanda. You know him better than I do and you've met him only twice. Yes, I know him, but not well. I've heard that he's as sharp as a tack, a sidewinder who never hesitates to bend the law to get what he wants, but he's also very careful, and that's about all I know."

"I take it that you *do* know Warren and Myers well?" she said, her eyebrows raised.

"Unfortunately, I do. I've had several run-ins with Warren, both in court and out. Once, on the golf course, we were in the middle of a round and I saw him move his ball. I called him out on it, and he flat out denied it, so he's a cheat and a liar as well. He's like that in court, too, and should have been disbarred years ago. Myers... I know him too, but not as well. He made an enemy of my father back in 2010. They were both trying to land a whale of a corporate client and Myers pulled some kind of sleazy shit and tried to put one over on August, but it didn't work; he caught it and Myers lost the client. To see them together at the club, you'd think they were the best of friends, but it's all bull. That's what I hate about lawyers; they're all damned bottom feeders. At least my dad has some redeeming qualities. He's honest, too; Myers isn't, and neither are the others."

I was beginning to get carried away, but then there was a knock on the door; it opened, and Jacque stuck her head in.

"Mrs. Nicholson will be here on Friday at noon."

I nodded. "That'll work."

"I've also confirmed with Doc Sheddon, and we have ten minutes with Assistant US Attorney Harrison at ten thirty tomorrow, and lunch with Heath Myers at the club at noon. Judge Warren hasn't returned my call yet. Are the appointment times okay?"

I told her they were, and she closed the door. I looked at my watch. It was almost three o'clock.

"Amanda, I need to call Kate. I have to get Nicholson's gun to forensics, and then I need to call August. Do you mind?"

She didn't, so I made the calls.

12

WEDNESDAY, JANUARY 11, 3:00 P.M

I punched the speed dial in my iPhone and waited. Kate answered on the forth ring.

"It's about time you called," she said. "Where the hell have you been?"

"Hello, Kate. Yeah, sorry. I've been busy working a new case." I spent the next few minutes filling her in on what I'd been doing for the past several days.

"I don't remember that case, sorry. I should, but I don't."

"Well, the reason you don't remember it is because it never was a case. It was deemed an accident, and it was county besides. But look, I need a favor."

"You always do. But that's okay. What can I do for you?"

"I have Nicholson's shotgun. I need to have Mike Willis take a look at it. Can you arrange that for me, please?"

"I'll need to run it by the chief, but it should be okay. He owes you, and more than one. Give me a minute."

She put me on hold for what seemed like a half hour. I was just about to hang up when she came back on.

"Sorry, Harry. He wasn't in his office, but I found him and he said it was okay. I called Willis and he said okay too, so why don't you bring it on over? I'll be here 'till six.

"Fine, and thanks, Kate. See you in a few."

I slipped the forensic and autopsy reports into a portfolio and then went to get Nicholson's Browning from the gun room. I said my goodnights to Jacque and the rest of the crew, and Amanda and I headed out. I told her to give me an hour and then meet me at the club, where we'd meet up with August. Then, as an afterthought, I went back to my office and grabbed the bag containing Peter Nicholson's clothing.

"So, you made it then?" Kate said. "I was about to give up on you."

I looked at my watch. It just after five thirty. I gave her a quizzical look; she shrugged.

"Long time no see," she said.

"Yeah, sorry. How have you been, Kate?"

She didn't answer. Instead she asked, "How's Amanda?"

"She's fine. She asked me to say hello."

She nodded. "So what have you got?" She looked at the paper-encased Browning.

Wow. She's got something on her mind.

I've known Kate a long time, more than sixteen years, in fact, since she was a rookie cop. She was my partner until I quit the force in 2008, and unofficially in one form or another ever since. She's a classic beauty, almost six feet tall, slender, huge hazel eyes and long tawny hair, and yes, there was a time when we had a thing going between us, but that's a whole 'nother story.

"Okay, out with it," I said. "What's wrong?"

"Other than all the dead people around here? Nothing."

"Kate, come on. What's on your mind?"

She looked at me, shrugged, then said, "Harry... I've had a rough day, that's all, and I just want to go home, take a hot bath, and drink a whole bottle of wine. You know how it is here. We had two shootings today, one a nine-year-old girl caught in the crossfire. She died at the scene. So let's get to what you need and then I can get out of here. I told Mike you were coming. He's waiting."

I nodded, and together we threaded our way through the meandering corridors to the labs.

Mike Willis had been heading up CSI operations at the PD even before I joined the force back in '97. I never did get used to dealing with him. Oh, he's a friendly guy —too friendly, some would say—but he's also a little eccentric, over talkative, and the second most intelligent man I've ever met, after Tim. In short, he's a genius, and the best at what he does. He's short, overweight, a little on the scruffy side—clean, but untidy; he keeps his hair in a man-bun, for Christ's sake—and his eyebrows are thick and bushy.

He was sitting at his desk going through paperwork when Kate tapped on his door. He looked up, stood up, and came to meet us.

"Harry, congratulations are in order, so I hear," he said. "Well done. I hope you'll be very happy. Now, what is it you need...? Ah ha. I see it. Evidence. Chain intact?"

He was referring to the chain of custody. I told him that it wasn't, that the gun had been in the position of Nicholson's mother for almost fifteen years.

"I'm afraid the chain on this one was broken more years ago than I can count. But the seals are still intact."

He pulled on a pair of latex gloves, took the gun from me, peered through the plastic window, checked the signatures and dates on the label, nodded, then said, "Do you mind?" even as he began tearing away the seals and the paper.

Bereft of its covering, the Browning was a thing of beauty. Almost fifty years old, it was in pristine condition, and even back in the day must have cost Nicholson a bundle.

"Oh, nice," Willis said, hefting the gun.

It didn't look like it had been fired much. The walnut stock and matching forearm were like new. The blue on the barrels and the engraving and gold inlay were in pristine condition; it made my Benelli look... well, like it had come from Wal-Mart.

"Who'd it belong to? How old is it, do you know?" he

asked, bringing it to his shoulder and squinting down the barrel.

"1968, I believe, and it belonged to a guy named Peter Nicholson." I gave him the very short version of the gun's history as he swung the weapon back and forth, up and down.

He nodded appreciatively. "It's been well looked after, that's for sure." He brought the gun down from his shoulder, turned it over, peered at the trigger housing, then took it by the barrels and squinted at the muzzles.

"There's blood here," he said, looking up at me.

"I know. I wanted to get your opinion on that. Nicholson supposedly fell on the gun and shot himself in the heart—contact wound...." He was already shaking his head. "I'd also like you to check it for blood spatter and prints."

"Blood spatter? Why?"

"For one thing, I don't think it happened the way they would have us believe."

"They? Who're they?"

I told him, and he looked sharply at me. "All three of them? You're kidding, right?"

I shook my head.

"Jeez. We sure as hell need to get it right, then."

He put on a Donegan OptiVISOR binocular magnifier and inspected the blood on the muzzles, shook his head, shoved the binocular up onto his forehead, and then sat down on the edge of his desk.

"You say he fell on this, and that the gun went off and killed him?"

I nodded.

"Nope. Couldn't have happened that way. For a start, the blood here—" he pointed to it, moving his finger along the length of the stain "—is smeared, as if somebody wiped it on." He looked at me quizzically.

"I think the gun was placed under him after he died," I said. "That would account for it, right?"

"It would, but—and I'll need to check—I also don't see any blowback on or inside the barrels. This is a very powerful gun, Harry. A contact explosion, and that's what we're talking about here, would throw out a significant amount of blood and tissue. Some of it would have gone into the barrels. I don't see any. But let me make sure."

He went to a cupboard and retrieved a spray bottle of what I assumed to be luminol and a small black light.

He lightly sprayed the ends of the barrels and turned on the light. Only the smear on the opposite side of the barrel reacted.

"Yep, it's as I thought. Nothing. This weapon was not in contact with the body when it was fired."

"How about the rest of the gun—the furniture, breach, and trigger guard? Any spatter there?"

"I'll look, but why would you think that there might be?"

"I don't think this gun killed him," I said simply.

He laid the gun on a nearby table on its right side and misted its entire length. He pulled the binocular back over his eyes and turned on the black light.

"Hmmm. There's a little on the edge of the trigger housing, but... well, let's take a look at the other side."

He repeated the process, then stood back.

"Oh yeah," he said, as he grabbed a Nikon camera from a shelf on the wall behind his desk. Then, holding the black light in one hand and the camera in the other, he took several pictures.

"What do you have, Mike?" I asked.

"High-velocity impact blood spatter: microscopic droplets, mist all over the right side of the stock, forearm, barrel, and breach. It's also been disturbed—smeared— here." He pointed to a spot on the forearm. "Somebody grabbed hold of it while the blood was still wet. How the heck did it get spattered like that? More to the point: Who grabbed it?"

"Mike," I said, "I think he was shot by someone else, with another gun. I think this gun was leaned against the stump of a tree. I found the stump. There's blood spatter on it too. From fifteen years ago. How's that for incredible?" I shook my head. "In your opinion, how far away from the wound would this gun have been for it to have received this amount of spatter?"

"Six, maybe eight feet."

"And the direction?"

He picked up the gun and laid it down against the arm of one of the chairs, trigger housing facing outward.

"Is this how you think it rested against the trunk?" he asked.

"Yes, I think so." I reached out and adjusted the angle a little. "But more like that."

"So," he said, lowering the binocular over his eyes, then stooping over the gun and turning on the black light. "The droplets are elliptical and some have tails and satellites.... I'd say... that the direction was slightly from left to right and slightly downward, almost horizontal." He nodded, satisfied.

"But that makes no sense," Kate said. "The victim would have had to have been on... oh."

"On his knees, or crouched down." Willis nodded. "Like this."

He took two steps away from the gun, turned, crouched, and pointed with his left hand toward the weapon. "See? This would roughly be the angle of the spatter." He pointed with the other hand. "And this would be the direction from which the shot was fired. I mean, look, these are only approximations. I'd need to see the wound before I could offer a definitive opinion, but you get the idea."

"Is there enough there for you to lift for DNA analysis?"

"I think so. Fortunately the gun has been kept in a paper sack, so the residue shouldn't be contaminated. Give me a minute. I'll need some fingerprint tape."

Two minutes later we had what we hoped would be four viable samples. I thanked him and took the envelope with the sample inside it from him.

"I'll get these off to Lindsey at DDC for analysis," I said. "How about prints, Mike? If someone grabbed the gun, there would be prints in the smeared blood, surely?"

"Well there aren't any. Whoever did it was probably

wearing gloves. It's just a smear. But give me a minute," he said, getting up from the crouch. "I'll dust it and see what we have, if anything."

He dusted the gun, then said, "There are prints, but they are all overlaid by the blood spatter. They probably are Nicholson's, but I'll need comparisons.... Oh," he said, as I handed him the copy of the autopsy report. "Right. There they are. Okay then. That should do it. I can do the comparisons first thing tomorrow and let you know. Anything else?"

"Yes, there is. I'd like you to take a look at the clothing he was wearing."

"What am I looking for?"

I shrugged.

He nodded. "I'll check it out. Anything else you need?"

"Nothing I can think of right now, but who the hell knows? If anything else comes up, I can count on you, right?"

"Always. Have a good one Harry, Kate."

13

WEDNESDAY, JANUARY 11, 4:30 P.M

I t was just after four thirty when Amanda and I arrived at the country club that afternoon. We'd taken both cars and were lucky enough to find two parking spots close to the clubhouse. August was already in the lounge. My dad's one of those larger-than-life figures who dominates any room he happens to be in; it wasn't hard to find him. He was seated, glass in hand, talking to Federal Judge Henry Strange and ADA Larry Spruce. The three of them had been friends for longer than I could remember, and friends of mine for more than a dozen years. We were golfing buddies—we played most Sunday mornings, even during winter—and professional allies. It was, I can tell you, a good team to be a part of, and I was especially glad to see them that day.

"Harry, my boy. Amanda, my love." August boomed as we walked into the lounge. "I thought you'd gotten lost. Larry and I were just about to go get something to eat downstairs, but this will do fine." The downstairs he was referring to was the Gentlemen's Grill and Bar. "But first," he said, slipping an arm around Amanda's shoulder and hugging her to him, "we need to get this lovely lady something to drink. George!" He didn't quite snap his fingers, but he might as well have. "A G&T for the lady—Bombay Sapphire, if you please—and a double Laphroaig—one ice cube—for my boy. Henry, Larry, same again?"

"Uh, no, not for me," Strange said. "I need to get on home."

"Oh that's too bad, Henry," I said. "I was hoping you and Larry would join us. I uh... I have something I'd like to talk to you about—the three of you, that is. How about it. Can you spare an hour?"

"Well now," Strange said, beaming. "Since you put it like that. Make mine a Laphroaig too, please, George, but just a small one, straight; no ice."

I won't bore you with what we had to eat that evening. Suffice it to say that it was exceptional, as it almost always is.

We talked while we ate; mostly they questioned Amanda and me about our extended trip to the Islands. It wasn't until the meal was cleared away and the coffee on its way that I finally was able to turn the conversation to Peter Nicholson.

"I had a visitor on Monday, Dad, a friend of yours, so she said. Helen Nicholson."

He was silent for a moment, looked at the other two, each in turn. I looked at them too. Their faces were serious.

"Ah," he said, finally. "So that's what this is about. You're not getting involved in that, I hope."

Now that was not exactly what I was expecting to hear.

"I already am."

He shook his head sadly. "I wish you weren't, son. I really do wish you weren't."

Strange stared down into his cup; Larry Spruce gazed out of the window.

"Well," I said, "I can understand that, but it is what it is. I promised the lady."

He sighed, shook his head, waved his hand in the air to get the bartender's attention, waited until he arrived and ordered a round of drinks, waited until George had gone to get them, then said, "Harry, do you have any idea who you'll be going up against?"

I nodded. "I do. I also know that one of them murdered Peter Nicholson."

That got their attention.

"Harry," Spruce said. "How can you know that? It was almost fifteen years ago. It was ruled an accident, by the sheriff's office and by the medical examiner."

"That's true," I said, "But they were wrong—either that or they knew and covered it up, all of them. The two detectives didn't like what they found, but they were pressured by Israel Hands to go along with the finding. I've already spoken to the surviving detective, Ron Fowler. He told me he never was happy with the finding."

"Harry," Strange said, "I know Ellis Warren better

than anyone. The minute he finds out what you're up to he'll slap you with every legal restraint he can think of. He'll rip you a new one... uh, sorry Amanda."

She smiled sweetly at him and said, "Judge Strange, I'm a journalist. I've heard much worse."

That brought a smile to all of their faces, even August's, but I could tell he was more than a little upset.

"Look," I said. "I know them too, all three of them. They're a nasty bunch of bas...." I paused, looked at Amanda. She was smiling. "They're not nice people," I finished lamely. "But come on. You guys have dedicated your lives to doing the right thing. Digging up the truth about what happened to Peter Nicholson is the right thing to do. And anyway, I need something to do."

"Okay," Larry Spruce said. "I'll bite. What makes you so sure it wasn't an accident?"

"I've been to the scene. I've looked at the photos. The scene looks staged to me; I just don't buy it. He supposedly fell on his shotgun and shot himself for God's sake. That's what Warren, Myers, and Harrison said that day, but that kind of thing just doesn't happen, and if it ever did, it would be a chance in a billion. Bowden, the ME, and Hands both took their story about what they thought had happened and used it to close the investigation down. There never was one. Amanda, tell them."

"Tell them what? All I could find at the station was a couple of minutes of raw footage. I was still at Columbia in 2001, but it seems their stories were good for us, too." She paused, turned to me and said, "Why don't you talk to Charlie? If anyone can help you, it's him."

"Pit Bull Charlie? I would... but he and I aren't on the best of terms. Not since he came sniffing around after that number you did on me."

That made them all smile, including Amanda. It was no secret that Amanda and I had gotten off to a rocky start.

"Rocky" my rear end. I couldn't stand the sight of her.

It was four years ago when she interviewed me, supposedly for an on-air profile—I'd made the national news for the second time and she was an anchor at Channel 7 TV. The profile turned into a hatchet job. Talk about tearing someone a new one; she did a hell of a job on me and I swore she'd never get the chance to do it again.

Ain't it funny how life has a way of turning things around?

A week after the piece aired, Pit Bull Charlie Grove, Channel 7's customer advocate—make that Channel 7's nosey son of a bitch—came bouncing into my office as if he owned the place. He was wanting to do a follow up, only it was me that did the following, with a boot up his ass as I tossed him out into the parking lot.

"I remember that piece, Amanda," Spruce said with a grin. "You were a bit hard on him, as I recall."

"Hard?" I asked. "Hard? She...." I looked at her. "She's more than made up for it since," I said with a wry smile. "And she's going to handle Pit Bull Charlie for me, aren't you, my love?"

"How about we do it together? It's time you two buried the hatchet." She saw the look on my face. "No, *not* in his head. Don't worry, sweetie. I'll handle him, but you need to talk to him yourself. Hearsay is not what you need, now is it?"

I had to admit she was right, so I agreed and asked her to set it up, and then turned the conversation back to the three stooges.

"Look," I said. "I know Judge Warren well enough. We've clashed a few times, and I can handle him. Harrison? Well, I've had drinks with him and his wife on occasion. All three of them are members here, but Myers.... I've met him too, more than once, but you know him best," I said, looking at August. "I'm having lunch with him tomorrow. What do I need to know?"

He thought for a moment, then said, "You need to know he's a sly son of a bitch, a liar, and that he has a violent temper. Be very careful what you say to him, and never meet with him alone. Always have a witness present, and take everything he says with a pinch of salt. I've run up against him four times. I beat him in court once, and forced settlements on him the other three times. He's never forgiven me for it. So you being who you are puts you at a disadvantage. Be careful, son."

I nodded, then I looked at Henry Strange, my eyebrows raised.

"You want to know about Harrison, I suppose," he said.

"You're a federal judge. You must have had dealings with him."

"Many times, and I don't like him, although I have to say that for the most part I've found him to be a straight shooter. He's an expert in financial and criminal law. He's a small man, and I'm not just talking about his build, although it applies. What I'm saying is, he has that chip on his shoulder, and he's mean with it. He's tough and he's a winner, Harry. You'll have your hands full with him... if you can get him to talk to you at all. Look. I have to go, but before I do I want you to know that I think you're right. Mrs. Nicholson, bless her, needs closure, or justice, especially if what you say is true. That being so, you can count on me for whatever help you need, provided you don't ask me to cross any lines. Now, I'll bid you all a good evening."

We watched as he headed out of the lounge and down the stairs, then Larry Spruce said, "Same goes for me, Harry. Whatever you need, provided it's on the up and up."

"Thanks, Larry," I said. "I appreciate it. "Dad, it's time we left too. I have an early start in the morning. We on for Sunday?" I was talking about our weekly outing on the golf course.

"Of course."

"How about you, Larry? Will you be able to make it?"

"As far as I know."

"Good. We'll see you both then."

An hour later we were back home on Lookout Mountain.

"Harry, are you sure you want to do this?" Amanda

joined me at the picture window and handed me one of the two glasses she was holding. "Your friends looked worried."

I continued to stare out of the window. It was a fine, cold, clear night. The sky was an unbroken field of stars. The city below, a carpet of twinkling lights. "Our friends? Yes, they're worried, and yes, I want to do it; I'm going to do it."

I slipped my arm around her waist and pulled her close; she put hers around mine, laid her head against my shoulder, and whispered, "I know."

14

THURSDAY, JANUARY 12, 9:00 A.M

Thursday morning turned out to be one of those rare winter mornings when you realize just how lucky you are to be alive. I'd made the outbound leg of my two-mile run in darkness, but as I came back through the gate it was getting light, and by seven dawn had broken in a blaze of yellow, pink, and orange, though the sun, a great red ball, had barely cleared the edge of the horizon.

I left home early that morning, determined to be in the office by eight, and I was, though Jacque and most of the rest of the gang, even Tim, had beaten me there and the place was already a hive of activity.

I grabbed a sixteen-ounce mug of coffee, went to my office, turned on the logs, and settled in for ten minutes with the Times Free Press, but it wasn't to be. My backside had barely hit the leather when there was a knock at the door and Tim walked in, grinning like a damned Cheshire cat.

I put down the newspaper, looked up at him, and sighed. "What is it?"

"Here you go," he said, dropping the plastic bag with the 8mm tapes on my desk and handing me a sleeve of DVDs. "All done."

"*All?*"

"Yup. They were all fairly short. I did half of them here last night, then took the rest of them home, along with an AVC cable, the Pinnacle device, and the software, and finished them there."

AVC cable? Pinnacle device? What the hell are those? Hah. Better if I don't ask. "Great, well done," I said. "Thank you, Tim. I'll get to them later. Right now...."

"Gotcha. I have other stuff I need to get done too. If you need me, you know where I am," and, much to my surprise, he walked out of the office, closing the door behind him. Usually I had to cut him off, or he'd go on and on and on.... It was who he was. I smiled after him, over the rim of my cup, then grabbed the DVDs and riffled through them. They all were neatly labeled with title and run time. I looked at my watch. It was almost eight thirty; no time to do anything with them now. I had an appointment with the medical examiner and I wanted to arrive early.

I picked up the phone and buzzed Jacque. "You ready to go?"

She was.

The Hamilton County Forensic Center on Amnicola is a small, unimposing, one-story building about a block away from the police department. The small forensic unit it houses is lorded over by my old friend Dr. Richard "Doc" Sheddon: a small, round-shouldered, heavy-set man in his late sixties, almost totally bald, with a round, jolly face, and an attitude to match. He was also a master of his craft, though for some reason I could never quite put my finger on, he also reminded me of Bilbo Baggins.

He was at his desk when we arrived, a cup of coffee in one hand, the corner of the spread-out daily Times Free Press newspaper in the other. I knocked on the door; he looked up, folded his paper, and stood up.

"Hey, Harry, how's it..." and then he saw Jacque. "Whoops. My bad. How are you Jacque? Harry, sorry I couldn't make it out to your wedding. From what I heard it must have been one heck of a wing ding. I know Leo Martan well; good friend; haven't seen him in years though. So, what is it you want to talk to me about?" All that, and never a pause to draw a breath or let me say a word.

I looked at him, stretched out a hand to Jacque, and accepted the file she handed me.

"Peter Nicholson," I said.

"Nicholson? Peter? Don't know any Peter Nicholson. I knew a Chester Nicholson. Heart surgeon at CHI Memorial. Good one too. Died about five or six years ago."

"Chester was his father. Peter died fifteen years ago. That's what I want to talk to you about."

"Hmm, bit before my time. Didn't know he had any children. I know Helen though. Lovely woman, lovely woman. Talk to me, Harry."

I stepped up to the desk, opened the file, and handed the autopsy report to him; he dropped back into his seat like a sack of potatoes and flipped quickly through it.

"Bit thin, isn't it?" he asked, flipping through it a second time.

I nodded, and laid the photos of the body in the forest and two of the wound taken during the autopsy side by side on the desk.

He picked them up one by one, peered at them closely, looked up at me, his eyes wide. I laid the incident report in front of him. He picked it up, read through it, looked up at me again, laid it down, went through the photographs one more time, and then the autopsy report. Finally, he laid it down, sat back in his chair and looked at me, then Jacque, then me again.

"You'd better sit down, both of you," he said.

I stepped away from the desk and took a seat next to Jacque.

"Accident?" he asked skeptically.

"You tell us."

He shook his head, looking worried. "I'm not sure I can, just from this." He waved his hand over the photos and paperwork. "It's.... It looks odd, Harry, but...."

"Odd? How does it look odd?" I asked.

He sighed, leaned forward, picked up one of the photographs, and stared down at it. "Why are you here, Harry? What's all this to you?"

"Helen Nicholson came to see me the other day. She says it wasn't an accident, that he was murdered. She asked me to find the truth. If it *was* an accident, fine. If not, she wants to know who killed him."

He nodded, slowly, without looking up. "As I said, it looks odd." He laid the photograph down and picked up another one, gazed at it for a moment, then turned it over and held it up so that we could see it. It was one of a half dozen taken in the forest that showed the body lying face-down on the trail, the gun stock sticking out from under the right arm.

He shook his head and said, "It doesn't look right. It's the gun. It shouldn't be there. Well, not where it is. You of all people should know that."

I nodded. He was right, and I did. I just wanted to hear it from him. "Go on."

"The report states the weapon was a 12-gauge shotgun, and that, I think, is what we see here. That's a very powerful gun. If you fire one, and you're not holding it correctly, what happens?"

I grinned at him. "You either get a very nasty bruise or you lose the gun altogether, or both."

"Right. Absolutely right," he said, nodding enthusiastically. "But that's not what happened, is it? So let's say that this man is ambling happily along the trail carrying his gun in one hand and his prize in the other. He trips, falls on the gun and kills himself. No! Not in a million *years*, Harry!"

He leaned back in his chair, folded his arms, and looked at me over his glasses.

"And?" I asked.

"First off, no matter how he was carrying the gun, he

would have been holding it only lightly. And the muzzle would be at his side, not pointed at his chest. *And* the blast would have wrenched the gun out of his hand and flung it several feet into the air, in one direction or another. He could not have fallen on it, no matter how he might have been carrying it. Second—and it's difficult to tell looking at these autopsy photos; some of them are a bit fuzzy—what we have here seems to be a contact wound, just above and to the left of the sternum. It's elongated, elliptical, and the direction appears to be downward and from left to right." He was staring at the image, slowly shaking his head. "He would have had to have jammed the butt of the gun into the ground and then fallen headlong onto the muzzle. Not possible, Harry. Not. Possible."

He leaned back, opened his desk drawer, and grabbed a large square magnifying glass. "Look here." He held the magnifier over one of the photographs so that I could see the wound through it. "Look at the edges, Harry. They look ragged. It's not easy to tell from this photo, but it looks to me like scalloping. If it is, it indicates that the shot had already begun to spread. Which means there was some distance involved. Not much, but enough."

I nodded slowly. "Okay," I said. "So what we have here is not a contact wound, but one that was caused by a shot fired from at least two feet, maybe more, right?"

"Mmmm, maybe. As I said, it's hard to tell. I'd need to see the actual wound to be sure. The determination of the range of fire becomes the most important aspect of our investigation."

"Okay. So make a guess. How far away, do you think, was this one fired?"

"A guess? I don't *guess,* Harry." He shook his head and said, "In this case—with the lack of any stippling or gunshot residue, and the scalloping... the range of fire appears to be between three and five feet."

That was what I wanted to hear. "That much? You're sure?"

He shrugged. "I wouldn't swear to it; I'm not a ballistics expert. But I've seen a fair number of these types of wounds. The amount of scalloping, if that's what it is, and the central hole is still compact.... Yes, Harry. I'd say three to five feet."

He paused.

"But as to what actually happened," he continued, "I have no idea. Could it have been an accident? If it was, it's a new one on me. No. This was no accident. What the hell were they thinking?"

"I don't know, Doc. I've been asking myself the same questions. I don't have any answers. I even went to the site. I may have found some DNA, on that tree stump you see in that fourth photo, but whether or not it's any good, we'll have to wait and see."

"Sorry, Harry. I wish I could help more, but I'd need to do a full autopsy, and get Snyder in ballistics to take a look at it, but that's out of the question... unless...." He shrugged.

"Unless I can get his mother to agree to exhume the body," I finished.

"That's about the size of it."

I stood up. So did Jacque.

"I'm seeing her on Friday," I said. "I'll ask her, see if she'll agree. If she will, will you do it? She'll pay you."

"Yes, of course, but she won't need to pay me. Just get me a court order."

I nodded. "Shouldn't be a problem if she agrees. Would you be willing to testify at the hearing?"

He looked down his nose at me, hesitated for a moment, then sighed. "Of course. There's no doubt that the man was murdered. Someone has to pay for that. I'll need you to leave this stuff with me so that I can draft a report for the judge."

"No problem. We have more in the car. Right, Jacque?"

"Three more sets."

I looked at my watch, then said, "We need to go. Look, thanks for taking the time. I have an appointment with Alex Harrison. He was with Nicholson when it happened, along with Ellis Warren and Heath Myers."

He let his breath escape in a rush. "Good luck with them. Let me know, Harry. I'll do what I can." He held out his hand. I shook it. So did Jacque, and we left him staring down at the photographs.

One down, three to go.

15

THURSDAY, JANUARY 12, 10:30 A.M

Assistant United States Attorney Alex Harrison was in his office in the federal building on Georgia Avenue just a couple of blocks from my own offices, but he was not in a good mood.

At my knock on his open door, he looked up from the papers on his desk, beckoned, pointed to the two guest chairs, and looked down again.

"Ten minutes, Starke," he said, without looking up. "You've got ten minutes. What is it you want?"

"Nice to see you too, Alex. This is Jacque Hale, my PA."

"Nine and a half minutes. Better get on with it."

"Okay, if that's the way you want to do it. I'm here to talk about Peter Nicholson."

That got his attention. He looked up at me, then leaned back in his chair, his hands gripping the edge of his desk as if he were about to push off from a boat dock.

Alex Harrison was not a particularly imposing man:

tall enough, fit, brown hair graying slightly, thin face, high cheekbones, thin lips. If you saw him in a crowd, you'd pass him by without a second look. In the courtroom, however, it was a different story. He was quick, decisive, thorough, and a winner.

"Peter Nicholson?" he asked, frowning. "I haven't heard that name in years. Why him? Why now?"

"I had a visit from his mother the other day. She thinks her son was murdered. I do too, and I also think that either you, Heath Myers, or Ellis Warren—maybe all of you together—killed him."

I was watching him closely. His face drained of color, his eyes narrowed, and his lips tightened.

"You're out of your f...." He looked at Jacque. "You're out of your mind, Starke. It was an accident. He fell on his gun, for Christ's sake. In 2002."

"There's no statute of limitation on murder; you of all people should know that, Alex," I said mildly, still watching his face.

He slowly shook his head, his mouth open slightly, his eyes still narrowed. "You've got to be kidding me. You seriously think that I could have killed him? I'm a US attorney, for God's sake."

"Not back then you weren't. You were a junior ADA."

He tilted his head back, stared up at the ceiling, closed his eyes, then opened them and looked at me angrily. "I should have you tossed out of here on your ass. The only reason I don't is because I know you're.... What the hell makes you think he was murdered?"

Ah ha, Alex. You want to know what I know. Well, let's see what we can do for you.

"It's pretty damned obvious if you have a half a brain in your head. All you have to do is look at these," I said. Jacque already had the file ready, and handed it to me before I had the chance to reach for them. I tossed the photos onto his desk in front of him.

"You're a criminal prosecutor," I said. "Tell me that scene wasn't staged."

I waited while he looked at them. Finally, he looked up, shrugged, and handed them back to me.

"Looks fine to me," he said confidently, but I could see by the look on his face that it didn't.

"You're telling me that you would be happy to go into court and testify that that scene is legit, that it hasn't been staged?"

"No, I'm not telling you that, because what you're asking is hypothetical; it will never happen. I was there. I saw it, just as you see it in those photographs. It wasn't staged. It couldn't have been. Besides, both the medical examiner and the sheriff signed off on it."

"Yes, that sick son of a bitch Hands did, after Bowden made his decision, and he shut it down right there and then; there was no investigation, no forensics, just a cursory autopsy as required by the state. It lasted all of fifty-five minutes for Christ's sake. They didn't even check the damn gun properly. The lead detectives didn't agree with Hands or Bowden," I said. "They both thought the scene was faked. I know. I talked to Ron Fowler. He never was happy about the way it was, thought the whole thing was, and I quote, 'covered up'...."

He didn't answer, so I continued. "Come on, Alex. Tell me what happened that day. Who found him?"

"Heath did. He found him lying there, just as you see in the photographs. When I arrived, Ellis was already there. He was on his knees, feeling for a pulse, but there was none, and no, he didn't move him. I called it in."

I nodded, my mind wandering, picturing the scene.

"So," I said. "Tell me about Judge Warren. Was he having an affair with Mary Ann Nicholson?"

We stared at each other across the desk. The man was not happy; in fact, he looked decidedly uncomfortable. He leaned forward. "I've had enough of this. Screw you, Starke. Your ten minutes are up. I'm not saying another word, and you'd better have more than these few photos and the deluded ramblings of an old man before you start throwing accusations around. You mention my name in public, in connection with this... this... *concoction* of yours and I'll sue your ass for every penny you have, you smug son of a bitch. Now get the hell out of my office."

So that was exactly what we did.

Out in the corridor, I punched the button for the elevator, looked at Jacque, and laughed.

"Well," I said. "That went well."

"You think? I'd say he's on the phone right now, warning his buddies."

"Of course he is. I'm banking on it that he is."

"But won't that let them know that we're onto them?"

"Yup. Better yet, it will start their juices flowing, wondering what we know and what we intend to do about it. You noticed the only information I gave Harrison was a look at the photos and that I thought the scene was staged. He took it and ran with it. You only had to look at his face to see that his brain was in overdrive. Always leave them wanting more, Jacque. That way you can always get them to talk to you."

"So you think it was him, then?"

"I think it *could* have been him. It's too early to draw any firm conclusions yet, and I'm quite happy to let him and his two friends stew for a while. Let's go have lunch with Myers, see what he has to say for himself…. How much would you like to bet that he's talked to Harrison and is ready and waiting for us?"

She smiled at me and shook her head. The elevator dinged, and the doors slid open.

16

THURSDAY, JANUARY 12, NOON

Heath Myers was indeed waiting for us when we arrived at the country club. So was my father. They were at the bar, talking together. Myers was leaning on the rail, glass in hand, trying to look nonchalant. He didn't. In fact his round, puffy face looked decidedly pale. Myers was maybe a year or two older than Alex Harrison, say forty-seven. He was a tall, overweight man with a spare tire that hung over his jeans and stretched the buttons of the blue-and-black flannel shirt almost to the breaking point. The jeans, shirt, Carhartt vest, and L.L.Bean rubber boots gave him a look that shouted construction worker, rather than the high-powered attorney I knew him to be.

"Hello, Heath," I said, and inwardly cringed as I did, because it came out sounding like Jerry Seinfeld's "Hello Newman." I felt Jacque's elbow in my ribs and, out of the corner of my eye, August smiling and turning his head away.

Myers looked at me like I'd just crawled out of the swamp at the rear of the seventh green. "Starke," he said. "Who's your friend? Amanda know about her? If she doesn't, she soon will."

"And on that note," August said, "I'll leave you to it. Harry, when you're done here, you'll find me in the bar downstairs." He slapped me on the shoulder as he passed by, still smiling. *Hello, Jacque,* he mouthed. She smiled.

"Jacque Hale," I said, grinning, "meet Heath Myers, attorney at law." I looked him right in the eye, and continued, "Heath is to the law profession what Ray Blanton was to Tennessee politics. Jacque is my PA and, yes, Amanda knows her well."

"That's slander, you piece of shit. I should sue your ass. Look, if you have something say, say it and get the hell out of my face."

"Tut tut, Heath," I said mildly. "First, it's not slander if it's true, which it is. Second, I have quite a few things to say, so how about I buy you a drink and we go sit down somewhere quiet and talk?"

"How about you stick your drink up your ass and we talk right here?"

I looked around, making a show of it. There were two waiters working the bar and four club members within earshot. "Well, if that's what you want, Heath..."

"Fine, you arrogant son of a bitch. There's a table over there, by the window."

I nodded, ordered a Blue Moon for me, a Campari and soda for Jacque, and nothing for my victim, who made his way to the table, parked himself with his back to the wall, and glared at me over his drink.

It took a couple of minutes for George to make our drinks. I could have had him bring them to the table. Instead, I decided to make Myers sweat. I turned my back to the bar, leaned on it, and stared back at him, a half smile on my lips. And yes, it was kinda funny. He sat very still, one hand holding his glass on the table. He looked calm enough, but I knew he was squirming on the inside.

Finally, our drinks were ready and I walked over to the table, put my glass down on it, and held out a chair for Jacque. I made sure she was nicely settled, then parked my own rear end right next to her; that put both of us facing Myers across the table, and I could tell he didn't like it. I didn't blame him. I'd set him up like he was about to be interrogated—which, I suppose, he was.

I picked up my beer, removed the orange slice, looked around for something to set it on.... Nothing. *Oh hell. Once can't hurt.* I dropped it into the beer, took a sip, and replaced the glass on the table. By now he was becoming decidedly antsy. I decided to put him out of his misery. Sort of.

"So, Heath," I said. "I know Alex called you—" the look on his face told me that I was right "—and that you know why I'm here. So let's get right to it. Which one of the three of you killed Peter Nicholson? Was it you?"

I thought his head would explode. His face grew even redder, his eyes became slits, and he visibly tensed; his knuckles whitened as he gripped the glass. I had to give it to him, though. He quickly got himself under control. He relaxed, sat back in his seat, and smiled at me.... Well, it wasn't really a smile; it was more of a snarl. It was a look that reminded me just what a dangerous, vicious piece of work Heath Myers really was.

I'm going to have to watch this one.

"You're one crazy son of a bitch, you know that? No one killed Peter. He tripped and fell and shot his own stupid self. He was a klutz, accident prone. Hell, I once watched him shut his hand in the car door, and I know he fell down the steps here at the club at least twice. It was an accident. The sheriff said so and so did the medical examiner."

"All you had to do was say no, Heath. Jacque," I said, holding out my hand.

She reached down and took the file from her portfolio and handed it to me.

"Okay," I said mildly. "Let's try to act like the grownups we are. You're an attorney. A bit sleazy, but a good one. Just take a look at these photos and tell me what you think."

I handed them to him. He took them, glanced quickly through them, then tossed them down on the table in front of me.

"As I said: an accident."

I shook my head in mock exasperation.

"Heath come *on*. Look, I'm not saying it was you that killed him, but *somebody* did, and there were only three people that could have done it: you and Harrison and Warren. Have another look." I picked up the top photo and threw it across the table at him. He flinched and let it fall to the floor.

"It's...." I paused, shook my head, then continued. "Whichever one of you arranged the scene to look like that wasn't the lawyer he is today. Jeez, Heath. It's the most obvious case of staging I've ever seen. You guys, one of you, maybe all three of you, got away with it then, but this is 2017 for Christ's sake. Look at it, man. Look where the damned gun is. It's a friggin' 12-gauge. There's no way it could have gone off and landed where it is, not even if he'd committed suicide, which he didn't. You know it and I know it. One of you placed it *right* there." I hammered my fingertip on the topmost image left on the table.

He sat for a moment, staring stoically at me, then looked at his watch, and then sighed and, seemingly without a concern in the world, asked, "You done, Starke? If not, please *get done*, because I have places to be."

I picked up my beer, leaned back in my chair, and stared at him, right in the eyes; he never flinched. He stared right back at me, an enigmatic smile on his lips.

Finally, he pushed his chair back and made to rise to his feet.

He was halfway up when I said, "Heath, was Ellis Warren having an affair with Nicholson's wife?"

He paused, still halfway out of his seat, seemed about to speak, but instead he stood upright, shook his head, and began to turn away.

"Okay," I said. "You win, but before you go, do me a favor...."

"As if," he snarled.

I smiled and nodded. "Yeah, I know, but take these with you anyway." I handed him the pile of photos. "And that one on the floor. Take another look at them and think on it. If you didn't do it, Heath, it had to be one of the other two. That puts you in a better position than me: I have three suspects; you, on the other hand, have only two. Look at the photographs. Which one of them do you think it is?"

"Screw you, Starke," he said angrily, and started to turn away, then he changed his mind and picked up the photos, including the one on the floor. He looked at me, screwed up his face, pointed at me with the bunched up photos, shook his head, and then turned and walked quickly out of the lounge and down the stairs. The man was in a hurry.

"What does that mean?" Jacque asked, once he was out of earshot.

"Not a damned thing," I said thoughtfully.

She shook her head. "I don't understand."

"I'm not sure I do either. He's one clever SOB, though, and nothing he does is ever as it seems. He's difficult to read; sly, wily, and a master of deception."

"But if he took the photographs, surely that means...."

"That he didn't do it? You might think so, but knowing him as I do, it could mean just the opposite, that he did do it and took the photos to throw us off track."

She nodded thoughtfully. "What do you think, Harry? Was it him, or Harrison, or the other guy? Wow, how do you do it? I'm so confused I can't see straight."

I smiled at her. "What do I think? Nothing yet. How do I do what I do? You know how. I observe and try to read people, suspects. I gather the facts, analyze them, sort through the evidence, use the science, and think it through, logically, step by step. My next step? I'm hungry. Let's go find August. I need him to do me a favor."

17

THURSDAY, JANUARY 12, 1:30 P.M

I t was almost one thirty when Jacque and I got back to the office. I asked her to try to get hold of Judge Warren, and then I told her to hold my calls. I was of two minds about what to do next. I needed to talk to Warren, and quickly. I debated whether or not to just head out the door and go visit him in his office, unannounced, and was about to do just that when Jacque knocked on the door and leaned in.

"Judge Warren is on the phone," she said. "He doesn't sound happy."

I smiled at her, nodded, and lifted the handset from its cradle.

"Ellis," I said loudly, my voice nothing but friendly. "I was hoping you'd call. How are you?"

"I didn't call. Your secretary called me. What the hell are you doing, Harry, digging up old trash?" He sounded reasonable enough.

"That must mean you've heard from Alex or Heath," I said.

"Both of them, damn it. I've had 'em both on the phone, and they're pissed, and I don't blame them. The Nicholson thing was put to bed more'n fifteen years ago. There's nothing there."

"You may well be right, Ellis, but Helen asked me to look into it and I said I would. Do you have a few minutes when I could come by and talk to you?"

"No, Harry. I don't. I have a full case load and I don't have time to revisit the long-dead past. You can say what you have to now, on the phone, then let me get back to the important stuff."

"Have it your way, Ellis. I've been to the site, and I've looked at the records and the photographs. It wasn't an accident. One of you killed him and staged it to look like it *was* an accident."

He was silent for a moment, then said, "That's a load of hogwash. I was there. I saw it. He tripped and fell. It's as simple as that, and after all this time there's nothing and no one to say any different."

"You're wrong, Ellis. I have a box full of evidence that says so, and the photos, the ones taken of the body. One of you shot him; that's a fact. Was it you, Ellis?"

"Goddamn it, Harry. Of course I didn't. We—Alex, Heath, and me—we were all together when we found him. Well, Heath found him first, but it was only by a couple of seconds. There's no way he, or any of us, could have killed Peter. It's... it's crazy, that's what it is. All you're going to do is stir up a whole hornet's nest of controversy and smear our reputations, and I won't have it. Do you hear?"

"Yeah, I hear you, but it's not enough. I'm convinced the scene was staged, and so is Doc Sheddon and Detective Ron Fowler. In fact, both he and his partner, Wade Brewer, said so at the time, but Hands and Dr. Bowden would have none of it. There wasn't even an investigation, for Pete's sake—no pun intended. Bowden took one look and that was it. Ellis, the man wasn't onsite even ten minutes, and Hands... well, you know all about him, right?" He didn't answer, so I continued, "I have the photographs, my own personal opinion of what happened, and four independent expert opinions to back it up. So I'll ask you again: Did you, or did you not conspire with Myers and Harrison to murder Peter Nicholson?"

"Not that I care, but are you recording this conversation, Harry?"

"No, Ellis. This conversation is just between you and me.... So, did you?"

"Not only no, but hell no."

"Okay, so let me ask you this: You married Nicholson's widow in 2004; were you having an affair with her when he died?"

"You... you son of a bitch. How dare you."

He didn't wait for an answer. He hung up.

I sat quietly for a moment, thinking. I'd spoken to all three men, and I still had no idea what had happened in Prentice Cooper that day. I looked at my watch. Almost two o'clock. I got up, went to get coffee, and then sat back down behind my desk. I sipped on the coffee and stirred the photos on my desk with my free hand, willing them to talk to me. They remained silent and, look as I might, they told me no more than I already knew.

I sighed and picked up the sleeve of DVDs and flipped through them until I found the one with Brewer's interview with Ellis Warren on it. I slipped it into the computer, clicked the mouse, picked up my cup of coffee, and then settled back in my seat to watch.

It was very short.

They were in an interview room, a much younger Ellis Warren, Brewer, and Fowler. Brewer did most of the talking; Fowler took notes, and Warren said as little as possible.

I ran the video through, then again, and then one more time. By the time the final run was finished, I'd figured that Warren owned less than two minutes out of the ten. He was asked to describe how they found the body, and he did so, in about a half dozen sentences. The rest of the questions he answered with a yes or a no or an I don't know. It was quite a performance.

It was basically the same story Alex Harrison had told me. They were supposed to meet at the trailhead at four o'clock that afternoon. Warren was on his way when he heard first one shot and then, a couple of minutes later, another. He figured it was hunters. Then he heard Myers shouting and he ran to see what was happening. He found Harrison and Myers standing beside the body just a short distance down the trail. Warren checked his vital signs while Harrison called it in. Myers continued to the trailhead by himself to meet the first responders. Warren and Harrison waited by the body. The sheriff's officers and TWRA showed up fifteen minutes later, the ME and an ambulance twenty minutes after that.

I ejected the disk and loaded in the one containing Myers's interview. It was almost identical. Only the verbiage was slightly different. I smiled to myself as I loaded up the third DVD, the Harrison interview; I figured I knew exactly what was coming, and I was right. More of the same. Coincidence? I didn't think so.

Sons of bitches. They got together and made sure their stories matched. Now why would they do that? Hmmm. Motive, that's what I need. Was Warren having an affair with Mary Ann Nicholson? If so, that might be a reason to off Peter. I wonder what Ronnie was able to find out.

I picked up the phone and buzzed him. "Hey, Ronnie. Were you able to do the financials I asked for?"

He had.

He walked into my office just a couple of minutes later with a laptop in the crook of his arm and sat down, still typing with his free hand. Finally he stopped and looked up.

"I just sent you a file. It should be on your desktop and iPad. It's pretty big, but I can give you the basics. You want to take notes?"

I did. I opened the desk drawer, removed a yellow legal pad, and set it in front of me.

"Shoot. What do you have?"

"Okay. So all four of them were heavily invested in the NASDAC when the bubble burst."

"Bubble? You're talking about that dot-com thing, right?"

"Yes. Are you familiar with what happened?"

"Eeeh, sort of. I know a whole lot of people lost a whole lot of money. The mechanics of it... no."

"Well then, I'll give you the short version. It all began in the mid–1990s. The Internet was coming into its own and people had begun to realize its potential for making money... mostly by selling things online. Companies were formed and some were wildly successful, some were not; nevertheless, most of them went public, so the NASDAQ became something of a rollercoaster. In 1996 the NASDAQ stock index was at six hundred; by 2000 it had reached more than five thousand, all because of the new dot-com companies, many of them run by kids barely out of college. It was a bubble because many of the companies lacked clear business plans—and some of the biggest companies had no earnings, and I mean *none*. Take Pets.com, for instance, an online pet products retailer. It was losing money even before it went public. When it did, it raised billions of dollars." He paused and shook his head. "They say that at the peak of the bubble in 1999, just before the collapse, a new millionaire was being created every sixty seconds.

"By early 2000, the reality was clear and investors realized that the 'dream' was a speculative bubble. By mid–2000, the NASDAQ was down more than three thousand points, close to two thousand. Panic selling ensued and the stock market's value lost trillions of dollars. By mid–2002, the NASDAQ had plunged to eight hundred. Hundreds of companies were wiped out. It was a time of great wailing and gnashing of teeth, and our four heroes were caught in the middle of it, big time."

"That's quite a story," I said. "So they lost money, a lot of money, right?"

"Two of them did, but—"

"Don't tell me. Peter Nicholson didn't."

Ronnie nodded. "Not only did he not lose money, he made a killing. How he saw it coming, I don't know, but he shorted several high-end stocks and cleaned up. Why he didn't tell his friends, I don't know.... Maybe he did tell them. Maybe they just didn't believe the bubble was about to burst. If so, they weren't alone. Many didn't, and lost everything."

"So how much did they lose?"

"Warren came off best. He wasn't as heavily invested as the other two, and he actually made money when the bubble burst. They were all into dozens of odd and ends, but most of their money was invested in two main stocks: Pets.com and Webvan.com. Warren lost his ass on Pets.-com, but he more than made up for it when he shorted Webvan; he ended up making almost $30,000, but Myers lost $72,000 and Harrison just under $90,000. Not vast sums of money, but these guys weren't wealthy, not then, and both Harrison and Myers had borrowed most of their investment capital. Myers, of course, has since made a fortune; Harrison, not so much, but he has managed to get free and clear."

"So, one way or another," I said, "all three had motive

enough to do away with him. How much was Nicholson worth when he died?"

"Not as much as you'd think. He made some good trades, like I said, but he also made a lot of bad ones. His net worth at the time of his death was just over $900,000, but that included the home, which was valued at $300,000. There were also the two insurance policies: one for half a million, the other for $750,00. Mary Ann Nicholson inherited everything. That's about it...." He paused for a moment, then said, "Like I said, Myers and Harrison recovered, though Harrison had taken out a second mortgage to cover his investment. He cleared that up, finally, in 2012. I pulled credit histories on all three. They're in good standing with scores ranging from 756— Harrison—to Warren's 803."

"Okay, thanks Ronnie. I'll take it from here, at least for now. Would you mind asking Heather to join me, please?"

"Heather," I asked as she took her seat, "were you able to find anything on Warren and Mary Ann?"

"Oh yeah, plenty," she said. "They were having an affair all right. Warren was married at the time of Nicholson's death. He has a son by his first wife. The son's name is Michael and he's twenty years old, still living with his mother. I spent some time with the ex-wife, Rachel. More about that in a minute, but first...." She flipped back and forth through several pages on her iPad.

"Before I talked to Rachel Warren I did a little digging. I made the rounds of the Nicholson's neighbors. It didn't long before it was pretty clear that something

was going on between Warren and Mary Ann. One lady
—" she paused and consulted her notes "—a Mrs. Pat
Lister, jokingly said that Warren spent more time at the
Nicholson home than Nicholson himself did. I say
jokingly, but then she went on to say that she may have
been exaggerating some, but it wasn't that far from the
truth. She saw Warren's car parked out front at all hours
—mornings or afternoons while Nicholson was at work,
evenings when he was out of town—so it seems they
didn't make it a big secret, but that all stopped after
Nicholson died, although his car was there almost
constantly the week after, then... only once in a while.
Maybe they got smart and decided to quiet it down for a
while." She reached for her glass of water, sipped from it,
then continued.

"Rachel Warren is... well, she married again back in
2009, to a Jonathan Stutz, but she hasn't gotten over what
happened to her. Warren dropped her like a hot rock;
divorced her in late 2003 citing irreconcilable differ-
ences. She never saw it coming. She knew that Warren
and Nicholson had been best friends since fifth grade,
that they were inseparable, so she thought little of her
husband spending so much time at their house. She said
that after Peter's death, Warren became reclusive, surly,
but again she thought she understood what was going on,
that he'd been deeply affected by his friend's death.
When he packed his bags and walked out of the door that
day she was, in her own words, dumbfounded. She tried
to talk to him, but he wouldn't see her, wouldn't answer
her calls or messages. She even turned up at his office a

couple times, but wasn't allowed in. The final blow came when he married Mary Ann. It was only then that she realized that they must have been having an affair, even before Nicholson's death, but for how long she couldn't even guess.

"Warren married Mary Ann in March 2004, just twenty-two months after Peter's death. They bought a house on Riverview, settled down, and kept a low profile. Over the next three years they had two children. The eldest, Catherine, was born in September 2004, just six months after they married. Ellis Jr. came a year later."

I sighed, dropped my pen on the pad, leaned back in my chair, threaded my fingers behind my neck, and stared up at the chandelier. It was a story I'd heard many times before in one form or another.

"There's more," Heather said.

"Oh yeah?" I asked, picking up the pen.

"I talked to some of Peter Nicholson's friends. It seems everyone knew about the affair but him, at least up until one of his friends and colleagues, Richie Dillon, filled him in. They were in the bar at Appleby's having an after-work drink when things turned, as they always do," she said dryly, "to the opposite sex. Apparently, Nicholson told Dillon that he hadn't had sex with his wife for six months, that she was always making excuses not to. It was then that Dillon told him about Warren. That was about a month before the so-called accident."

"No kidding?" *I've heard that one before too. Everybody in town knows about it but the poor sucker whose spouse is screwing around.*

She nodded. "Apparently Dillon was his shoulder to cry on. They met several times over those final four weeks, and Dillon says that Nicholson told him that he had confronted his wife and given her an ultimatum: it was either him or Warren. He also told him that they'd had one hell of a bust up, but that in the end she'd chosen him and promised to break it off with Warren."

"Wow. What about Warren? Did he confront him too?"

"I asked Dillon that, but he said he didn't know. He also said he doubted it, because Nicholson was a wimp—his words—and didn't like confrontations."

"So," I said, thinking out loud. "If Mary Ann had indeed broken it off with Warren...."

"Yep. Motive. I'd say Warren was hooked and wasn't about to give her up."

I nodded. I knew Warren well, and he wasn't used to being told no. *So why would Nicholson agree to go hunting with him? I wondered. I guess old friendships die hard, and he must have believed that the affair was over, that his wife's promise was good, and he was willing to forgive them both.... One thing is sure: they ended up in the forest together and Peter Nicholson died. But was it Warren who killed him? All three of them had motive, means, and opportunity. How the hell do I figure it out now after all this time?*

Motive? Only Warren had something to lose: Mary Ann. The other two had already lost a bunch of money—so revenge would be their motive; Warren had made money, so that wasn't it. But Mary Ann? Maybe that was it. Hmmm. So Warren then? Yeah, but....

"Okay, Heather. That will do for now. If I need you, I'll give you a buzz. Well done. I appreciate it."

She nodded, got up, and left me alone with my thoughts.

How? How? How? One of them ambushed the poor son of a bitch. The most likely suspect is Warren. He sure as hell has the temperament for it, and he was the only one with something to lose, but the other two.... Back then ninety thousand was a whole lot more money than it is today, and so was seventy-two grand, so rage, revenge....

I stared down at my notes. They helped, but not enough. I still knew only two things for sure: Peter Nicholson's death was no accident, and only one of three suspects could have killed him. *One more thing: how the hell did Warren manage to make money when the other two lost so much? And if Nicholson gave Warren the heads up, why not the other two? That alone would have made Myers and Harrison angry enough to kill.*

I had almost no evidence, no science—yet—but I did have motives, which didn't help a whole lot because they all had at least one.

I picked up the remaining DVDs, then put them down again. *Time for those later.*

I grabbed the cardboard box containing what little evidence there was and dragged it closer to me. I looked inside, took out the forensics report and the baggies containing the spent and live shotgun shells. The bag contained two smaller bags, each containing 12-gauge cartridges. The smaller of the two contained just two shells: both Winchester—one spent, the other live; both were 2¾-inch, 1¼-ounce number fours. The label on the bag stated they had been taken from Nicholson's gun. The label was signed by Lieutenant Wade Brewer. The other bag contained eight live shells, also Winchester, and identical to the two in the smaller bag. The label stated that these had been taken from Nicholson's right vest pocket. It was also signed by Brewer.

I dropped both bags into the box and picked up the plastic bottle containing shotgun pellets. I hefted it, turned it over and over in my fingers, then sighed and dropped it into the box. I looked at my watch. It was already after five; I'd had enough. It was time I went home, and I did.

18

FRIDAY, JANUARY 13, NOON

I woke early that Friday morning to yet another rainy day. No run for me. I left Amanda sleeping, showered, sat down with a cup of coffee in front of the picture window and looked out into the darkness and gloom; we were once again enveloped in a thick, heavy mist, up in the clouds, and I began to wonder if maybe I'd made a mistake moving to the top of the mountain. Then I remembered what it was like on good days.

Nah!

I hadn't been sitting there long when a pair of hands slipped over my shoulders from behind.

"Hey you," I said, without turning. "It's only five thirty. What are you doing up this early?"

"I missed you," she said, massaging my shoulders. "I was waiting for coffee, but you didn't bring me any."

"I didn't want to wake you." I turned in my chair to face her. She was wearing red-and-black striped satin pajamas from Victoria's Secret; what she didn't have on under them was no secret at all. I turned further, slipped my arm around her waist, and pulled her down onto my lap.

"Hey," she growled. "Coffee. I need coffee, and I haven't cleaned my teeth yet. My breath smells like an old dog's."

I kissed her anyway. "'Old Dogs and Watermelon Wine.' Tom T. Hall sang that, I think. No, honey. An old dog you definitely are not." I kissed her again, and she giggled and wriggled out of my grasp.

"Coffee first," she whispered in my ear, "and then we'll begin the day with a...."

I thought she was going to say "with a bang," but she didn't finish the sentence. If she had, it would have been an understatement. We hadn't been married more than a few weeks, but I already knew it suited me well. Amanda? She never said, but nor did she ever complain. Coffee? Yes. Breakfast? No.

She decided to come into town with me that morning. We took one car. I drove. The mountain road was a bear, more raging river than asphalt, and foggy to boot. It was a relief to finally emerge onto Broad Street. From there, however, even in the rain and rush hour traffic, with a quick stop at my father's house to pick up some papers I needed, it was an easy twenty-minute drive into the office. There Amanda took the car and headed for Channel 7.

As always on Friday morning, I called the staff together in the conference room for a breakdown of the work in progress for the week so far.

Aside from my own case, it was all routine, quickly dealt with and put aside, and to be honest, I wasn't that interested anyway. I trusted my team, especially after having left them alone for six weeks. That being so, I left Bob and Jacque to handle the meeting, poured myself a fresh cup of coffee, and retreated to my own office. I needed to think.

Jacque, bless her, had already turned on the fire and the room was quiet, just as I like it, but for some reason I couldn't relax. After ten minutes and a cup of coffee I went to my desk and picked up the bag of 8mm video-tapes from the box.

I set aside the three I'd already watched, the interviews of the three suspects, and sorted through what was left: three that documented the crime scene in detail— *Yeah, that's what I'm calling it: a crime scene*—one of Detectives Brewer and Fowler onsite taking the initial statements from the three witnesses, and two more documenting their own and Dr. Bowden's cursory inspections of the site and his interview by Brewer.

I inserted the Brewer/Fowler disk and watched as the two detectives went through the motions of interviewing the three men. They talked to them as a group. Fortunately, the camera operator had a sense of what he was supposed to be doing, but the video quality was poor and the sound was... well, maybe the wind was blowing; it certainly sounded like it.

From time to time, Sheriff Israel Hands could be seen standing at the perimeter of the site, watching the proceedings like a malevolent crow. It was obvious he was there only because he had to be.

Both detectives asked questions of the group, and both took notes. *I wonder what happened to those,* I thought as I sorted through the box, knowing damned well they weren't there.

Brewer took the lead; Fowler did his best to dig for information but the old man, Brewer—he had to be close to retirement even then—was constantly cutting him off, nodding his agreement as the three mouseketeers did their best to convince him it was an accident. Hmmm. Had Brewer been in on the fix, I wonder?

I ejected the DVD, slid it into its pouch, and flung it down on the desk. *What a damned fiasco.*

The Bowden disk was no better. Bowden wandered around the body, both hands in his pockets, head bowed, looking for all the world like Winston Churchill the night after one of his famous binges. The only time he got closer than six feet to the body was when he bent down to feel for a pulse. He did speak at some length to Ellis Warren, though what passed between them is anybody's guess; it certainly couldn't be heard. Warren talked and Bowden nodded, glancing now and again at the body. Finally, he nodded, leaned in close to Warren's ear, said something, clapped him on the arm, then turned and walked away. I watched in awe what had officially been deemed the medical examiner's inspection of the body and the site.

The next video was a little better, barely. It showed Brewer and Fowler already onsite. They were alone with the body, but again the sound was overwhelmed by a discordant electronic hiss that made the words unintelligible. *I wonder if Tim could do something with it. Hah, at least they're wearing gloves.* And that was all they were wearing: no booties, no coveralls. They wandered around the body together. Brewer seemed to have little to say, but Fowler, I could tell, was asking questions to which the answers were obviously yesses and nos. Fowler did spend some time crouched beside the body seemingly checking out the gun, and he did look several times along the body in the direction of the trailhead, and back along the trail too. He stared at Nicholson's boots, but he didn't touch them and, on a couple of occasions, looked at Brewer and spoke to him loud enough to be heard by the camera.

"You think this looks right, Wade?" The only answer he got was a shrug. "I don't like it. There's something weird about the gun. What do you think?" Again the shrug and a reply I couldn't hear, but Brewer was shaking his head as he spoke.

So they really did think there were problems.

The video ended. I played it again. Then I played the interview scene again. This time I watched closely; I watched the faces of the three men as they told their story and this time I knew they were just going through the motions, all three of them. I couldn't hear what they were saying, but I could see them speaking: they were stone-faced, expressionless... emotionless, and that was not how people are when a friend has been killed. I watched the video through a couple more times before I finally ejected it and reinserted the Brewer/Fowler tape. This time I watched Brewer's face.

I'm not going to tell you the man had a personality, but compared to the three stooges, he was animated.

Sheesh!

HELEN NICHOLSON ARRIVED JUST before noon. Jacque showed her into my office and offered her coffee, which she declined, and then Jacque turned to leave.

"I'd like you to stay, Jacque," I said. Mrs. Nicholson looked surprised, but she said nothing and I didn't explain. "Let's sit over here. It's more comfortable."

I took the chair on one side of the coffee table; Jacque and Helen Nicholson sat together on the sofa opposite.

"First," she said. "I won't be able to stay for lunch. I have an appointment. Second, I'd like to know what progress you've made, if any."

"Some. Some." I paused. *Oh boy. This is* not *going to be easy.*

I decided to answer her question and then ease into it, but before I could:

"Ms. Hale—" she turned her head to look at her "—said you need my DNA. May I ask why?"

"You may," I said. "You'll remember that we found blood on the tree stump. I think it's Peter's but I can't be sure unless the lab has a reliable comparison. We don't have Peter's, but we do have yours, and that will work fine...." I paused, unsure of how I was going to say what needed to be said next.

"I've gone over what little evidence there is, and I've talked to Detective Fowler and Dr. Sheddon. We are all of the same opinion: your son was murdered. The problem is proving it. Yes, everything points to it, and there's expert opinion to back it up. That being said, there will also be plenty of experts who say the opposite. We all feel that the wound was not made as a result of contact with the muzzle of the weapon, that he was shot by someone standing several feet away from him, but to prove that...." I hesitated. *Here we go.*

"Well, go on."

"We need a second autopsy of the body."

Her mouth dropped open; the color drained from her face. She stared at me across the desk.

"You want to disinter him?" It was barely more than a whisper.

"Yes."

She shook her head violently. "No. *No!* I can't allow that."

I leaned forward, my elbows on my knees, hands clasped together. "I know how you must feel...."

"No. No you don't," she said quietly, staring down at the carpet. "You have no idea how I feel.... I can't... I won't allow it." She looked up at me, her face set.

I leaned back in my chair and nodded.

"Mrs. Nicholson," Jacque said, placing her hand on her arm. "There's no other way. The photographs are inconclusive. Dr. Sheddon and Ms. Snyder must be able to examine the wound."

She snatched her arm away. "Snyder? Who's Snyder?"

"She's a ballistics expert; very good at what she does."

There were tears rolling down Mrs. Nicholson's cheeks. "I can't do it, Harry. I just can't. He's... he's with Chester. In the same plot. It would mean disturbing both of them."

She took a tissue from her coat pocket and wiped her eyes; her mascara had run, and she had two black eyes.

"Well," I said, "I understand how you feel. I'll do what I can, but...."

Can I use the restroom, please?" she asked. Already rising to her feet. "I need to clean up."

"Of course. My private bathroom is through that door. My wife keeps some things in the right-hand cupboard. Help yourself."

She nodded, looked disconsolate, went to the door, opened it, looked back at me, hesitated, and then closed it behind her.

"Well," Jacque said. "That's that, I suppose. What now?"

"Now we give her a little time to think. Maybe she'll come around."

As it happened though, we didn't have to give her time at all. She emerged from my bathroom some ten minutes later, her face set, grim.

"You really think it's necessary?" she asked, sitting

down again, crossing her feet and folding her hands in her lap.

"I do," I said.

"Then do it. I have to know who killed him, and I want them to pay for it. How do we do it?"

"I need you to sign this for me," I said, handing her the petition I'd had my father draw up the evening before.

She leafed through the three pages. "What is it?"

"It's a petition to have Peter exhumed. I had August draw it up last night. He's also agreed to represent you in the matter, if that's all right with you."

It must have been, because she asked for a pen and, without another word, scribbled her signature and initials in the appropriate places and rose to her feet.

"I have to go," she said quietly. Jacque opened the door for her, but she turned to look at me in the doorway. "You'll keep me informed?"

"Of course. As soon as I know something—" But she closed the door before I could finish, leaving Jacque and me staring at the polished wood.

"What now?" Jacque asked.

"Now we get this into the hands of a judge." I looked at my watch. It was not quite one o'clock. "Let's go," I said. "The quicker we get this done the better. The minute Warren gets wind of it... well, things will hit the fan."

We walked the four blocks to the courthouse on Market Street and went straight to the criminal court clerk's office, where I handed the petition to the clerk

himself, John Hammond, a man I'd had plenty of dealings with over the past ten years.

He looked at it, looked up at me, looked at it again,
then said, "You can't be serious."

"As a heart attack."

"I remember this," he said. There was a look that
could only be described as awe on his face. Then he
smiled. "I'm going to enjoy this, Harry. Can't wait to see
the look on Warren's face when he finds out. Might just
have to tell him myself."

"When can you get it in front of a judge, John?"

"This afternoon. I'm thinking Judge Harris. He has a
full docket, but he's the one you need, and he's no friend
of Warren's. I'll call you when I know something."

And he did, later that afternoon. The hearing was set
for Wednesday February 1 at ten in the morning.

And now we wait.

19

SUNDAY, JANUARY 15

I played golf with my father that Sunday morning. The weather was fine and the course was in the best condition I think I've ever seen it in winter. As usual, Henry Strange and Larry Spruce completed the foursome; I partnered with Larry. The stakes were high: ten dollars on the game, two-dollar birdies, and free drinks for the winners. And, as usual, it was August and Strange that walked off the course as the winners, but only by a single hole. Birdies were even, so the tally was that Larry and I had to hand over a ten-dollar bill each and open a tab for the drinks, which we did.

Amanda and Rose were already seated in the great bay window that overlooked the ninth green. Henry and Larry would stay for a couple of drinks, then head on home; we almost always had Sunday lunch at the club, and it was the plan that day too.

"So, Harry." Strange leaned back in his chair and stared at me over his glass, a wry smile on his lips. "Once again the city is abuzz with your exploits. You do like the limelight, don't you?"

"Not especially. You're talking about the petition, I guess?"

"Right. Do you have any idea of the stir you've caused? No? Amanda—" he turned to look at her; she tilted her head, eyes questioning "—I'm surprised you haven't been dragged into it. The media is all over it."

"They are?" I asked. "I haven't heard anything."

"You will, Harry my boy. You will."

I looked at August. "Have you heard anything?"

"Only around here."

Involuntarily, I glanced around the room. I saw no evidence of untoward attention. At least not then. I was in no way ready for what was to come.

Less than ten minutes later, a whirlwind arrived, followed by a tempest of cosmic proportions. An obviously irate Mary Ann Warren stormed toward us from across the room, followed by her equally angry husband.

"What the hell do you think you're doing?" She didn't quite yell at me, but she might as well have; every head in the room turned to look at her.

"Hello, Mary Ann," I said. "Can I get you and Ellis a drink? I already have a tab open."

It was as if I'd poured gasoline on a raging fire. Her face, already red, turned puce. I was suddenly worried she was about to have a heart attack.

Larry Spruce was sitting right in front of where she was standing and, fearing for his own safety, he moved his chair to one side and gazed up at her. He opened his mouth to speak, but changed his mind and closed it again.

She took another step forward, into the space that Larry had just vacated; she was now less than three feet away from me, and I was now worried she was going to try to do me physical harm. I couldn't help but be impressed by her presence—and by her beauty, too, even as angry as she was.

Her three-inch heels made her even more imposing, that and the way she was standing: feet apart, hands clenched into fists on her hips.

"You've petitioned the court to have my husband exhumed, you son of a bitch," she snarled.

"Whoa. Easy now," August said. "That's my son you're talking to and his mother, God rest her soul, was no bitch. Try to keep a civil tongue, woman. Ellis. You need to put a stop to this, right now."

But there was no stopping her. Nor was Ellis disposed to try. He simply stood behind her, his lips pulled back, his teeth bared.

"Your husband?" I asked quietly. "I thought Ellis was your husband."

"You know what I mean. Why? Why would you do such a thing after all these years? Peter's death was an accident."

I was tempted to stand and face her, but I really didn't want to dignify her argument, or her.

I looked up at her, glanced around her at Ellis, then said, quietly, "I'm acting on behalf of Peter's mother—"

"You *can't*. I'm Peter's next of kin, not her. You need

my permission, and you can't have it. I won't have you disturbing him."

"In normal circumstances you'd be right, Mary Ann: only you could petition to have Peter exhumed, but these are not normal circumstances. You see, I don't think it *was* an accident, and neither does the Hamilton County Medical Examiner, or Sheriff Walker. That, along with newly discovered evidence, requires a medical examination to establish the true cause of death. I think he was murdered... by one of his friends."

I was watching Ellis closely as I said it, and I thought for a minute he was going to explode. Instead, he took his wife by the arm and pulled her away, then stepped forward into her place.

"What new evidence? There is none. I was there."

"That's for me to know and you to find out," I said easily. "You say you were there? Maybe you were; maybe you killed him. If so, we'll figure it out. I do know this: if your friend Israel Hands had allowed his detectives to do their jobs back then, one of you, maybe all of you, would be sitting in jail right now. Well, it's not too late to find out the truth, which is all Mrs. Nicholson wants... but—" I smiled up at him "—as you well know, *Judge,* there's no statute of limitations on murder."

He was all but apoplectic. "You bastard, you—you—you piece of.... I ought to smack you right in the mouth, you arrogant, self-righteous son of a bitch," he snarled. He was so angry he could barely spit the words out.

I twisted in my seat, shook my head, and looked up at

him. He hadn't yet invaded my space, but I was ready for him if he did.

"Ellis," I said with a sigh, "you really should be careful who you threaten, especially in front of witnesses, and even more especially when the person you're threatening might hurt you... a lot, if you were stupid enough to try. Now why don't you take your... take Peter's next of kin and leave us to eat our lunch in peace."

The next of kin didn't like that one bit. *"How dare you,"* she screeched, then seemed to realize where she was. She looked around the room. It was a sea of grinning faces—the Warrens were not a popular couple.

"How dare you," she repeated, lower, but no less furiously. "I loved Peter dearly. He was my *life*. I was *devastated* when he died, and it *was* an accident. The sheriff and Dr. Bowden both said so. It's on the death certificate."

I should have kept my mouth shut, but I couldn't help myself. "You loved Peter? He was your life?" I was shaking my head in disbelief. "You have the gall to stand there with his *best friend,* who you married less than two years after his death, and tell me that?" I didn't wait for them to answer. "How about this? How about I have sworn statements from witnesses that state you two were having an affair at least a year before your husband died, and that he knew it, and that he'd threatened to divorce you if you didn't break it off with him?" I waved a hand in Ellis's direction and stood up. I was angry now.

They both backed away a step. The room was silent, and so were the Warrens.

They stood for a moment, staring at me wide eyed. Then Ellis took her arm, pulled her away, and steered her out of the door and down the stairs.

I watched them go, then sat down again. I had a horrible feeling I'd gone too far, way too far, especially in front of the members.

"Well," August said, waving a hand to call for drinks. "That was interesting."

Judge Strange emptied his glass. "It was indeed."

For a moment, everyone at the table was quiet, then Rose put a hand to her mouth and burst out laughing.

"Well," she said, through her fingers. "Why didn't you tell them how you really feel, Harry?"

I shook my head, grimaced, then smiled. "I have a feeling I haven't heard the last of them."

I was right.

20

MONDAY, JANUARY 16, 9:00 A.M

Henry Strange was right about the media, as I found out when I arrived at my offices the following morning. I hadn't been inside more than a couple of minutes when the front door opened and in walked Channel 7's Charlie Gove—Pit Bull Charlie, to those who know him well, which I did. He was, or had been, one of Amanda's closest allies and friends during the years she'd worked at the station. Why, I had no idea.

He was a mean little man, short but in extraordinarily good shape, and clean-shaven except for a prematurely white mustache that made it look like he dyed his shock of dark brown hair, which he didn't.

I'd never really liked the man, though I could think of no good reason why. He was always friendly toward me, and had treated Amanda with respect, though I did have an idea he had a thing for her. I'd even mentioned it to her once, but she'd simply laughed and said the idea was preposterous. Maybe for her.

I shouldn't have been surprised to see him, but I was.

"Charlie," I said, offering him my hand. "Long time no see. To what do I owe this rather dubious pleasure?"

"Come on, Harry. You're back in the news again. In the past it would have been Amanda, but following your recent nuptials, any reporting she might do where you're concerned would be a conflict of interest. Besides, she doesn't return to work until after the first, and she said it was okay for me to talk to you. So here I am. Ready to listen or do battle, whichever you prefer."

I couldn't help but smile. Charlie was nothing if not forthright. A loudmouth, nosey son of a bitch, he was, in Amanda's words, "about as popular as a wet dog at a wedding." Be that as it may, he was extremely good at what he did, which was to put the screws, on air, to any and all businesses, small or large, that he felt might have taken advantage of one of Channel 7's viewers. Just a hint that Pit Bull Charlie was sniffing around was usually all it took to bring justice to the masses. Love him or hate him, he got the job done, and he brought in the ratings.

"Okay, Charlie," I said. "I'll bite. What is it you want?"

"I want the skinny on your Nicholson investigation— you want to dig him up, so I understand—and I want the exclusive you would have given to Amanda."

So Henry was right. The word was out and Charlie, I was sure, was just the first.

"You do, huh?" I looked at him, appraising. *This might be an opportunity.* "How about some coffee?"

"Sure. Why not. Decaf, please."

So I made him a cup. I made myself sixteen ounces worth—of Dark Italian Roast, black—and we headed to my office.

"Take a seat, Charlie," I said, as I dropped heavily into the throne behind my desk. He did.

I tilted my chair back as far as it would go, held the big mug in both hands, and stared across the desk at him.

"Charlie," I said thoughtfully. "I don't mind giving you an exclusive, might take some of the heat off me, but...." I paused.

He waited.

Savvy son of a bitch.

He kept waiting.

"Well," I said, "Charlie, I could always rely on Amanda to...."

"Spin things the way you wanted them? That's not me, Harry. I tell it like it is; always have. If you're not happy with that... well. Tough."

He sipped on his coffee, watching me as I thought about it.

"No, that's not what I want. It's just, two things: if I give you what you want, you can't broadcast anything unless and until I say you can. Agreed?"

"Hmm... I suppose. Agreed. What's the second thing?"

"I know you, Charlie. They don't call you Pit Bull for nothing. You're like a dog with a bone. You never give up. You'll dig and dig. You'll get into places I can't go, and find out things I never would be able to. I want you to share those things with me... and other than me, I want you to keep them to yourself and, per our agreement, broadcast nothing of it unless I give you the go ahead."

Oh, that made him unhappy, but I stopped him before he could object.

"I know, I know; that's not the way you do things. Well, if you want me to cooperate with you, it is now. Think of it as being a part of the investigation. You can even take some of the credit; Amanda always did, as well you know. Come on, Charlie. When you know what I know, you'll be one happy pit bull. What do you say? This could be a big one for you."

He stared at me. I could almost hear the wheels turning inside his head.

Finally he looked down at his cup, then up at me, and said, "Deal. Let's talk."

And we did.

I had Jacque join us—she already knew Charlie quite well—and then I spent the next thirty minutes filling him in on what we knew and where we were with the investigation. He already knew the official version of what had happened that day in 2002, but he had no idea how Hands and Bowden had shoved the accident theory into the records, and when I showed him the evidence he couldn't believe it had happened.

"Charlie," I said finally. "I'm deadly serious. No one outside of this office except for Doc Sheddon, Amanda, and my father, who drew up the exhumation petition, know what you now know. If any of it leaks, I'll know it was you, and I'll shut you out. You hear?"

He heard all right, and he nodded, but I could tell his

mind was on the enormity of what he'd gotten himself involved in.

"Harry," he said. "Warren *was* having an affair with Mary Ann Nicholson, but about two weeks before he died she called it off."

I stared at him. "And you know this because...."

"When I heard you were looking into Nicholson's accident, I did a little digging—yeah, yeah, I know. Anyway, I talked to their neighbors too. I also talked to some of his friends. He was a popular guy. Played a lot of golf. He always played with the same three guys... no, no, not those three. Three other guys. Anyway, I talked to two of them—the third wouldn't give me the time of day. It seems that on the Wednesday two days before the accident, the four of them were in the male-only bar. I can't believe they still have one of those." He shook his head, then continued.

"Anyway, they got to talking, and drinking, and Nicholson had a few more than was good for him and he told them about Warren and his wife, and apparently he was pissed off, and I mean *really* pissed off. He told them he'd only known about the affair a few weeks, but he'd put a stop to it; threated to divorce her unless she quit fooling around."

Hmmm, so Heather was right. Now we have it from a different source. Peter Nicholson did know about the affair.

"I knew she'd supposedly called it off," I said, "but what we don't know is if he confronted Warren."

"Yeah, we do," he grinned. "From what my sources

tell me, they had a 'gentlemanly conversation'—Nicholson's words—a week before he died. Apparently Nicholson told Warren he was willing to forgive and forget, but that if Warren went near his wife again, or contacted her in any way, Nicholson would ruin him."

"Whoa, that's new. Did he say how he would do it?"

"He didn't tell his golfing buddies, but he did let it out that Warren wasn't the squeaky-clean attorney he made himself out to be. Sounds to me like he had something on him, yeah?"

"Yeah," I said thoughtfully, "but what?"

"I don't know, and honestly, I don't know if there's any way to find out after all this time."

"Okay, so let's think about it for a minute," I said. "It couldn't have been Warren's womanizing. Everyone already knew about it. So what else is there?"

"Money." We both said it together. And then we were both silent.

"It's always the money," I said.

"Yeah, but how?"

"Well, we know he's a greedy, rich bastard. We also know he was heavily involved in stock trading and that Nicholson was his broker. You remember the Dot-com thing, right?"

"Oh yeah. Got caught in that one myself, as did everyone else I know."

I smiled at him, nodding.

He looked puzzled, tilted his head, and screwed up his eyes; the question was there but unasked, and then he got it.

"No. Not Warren."

I nodded. "Yep. I had one of my guys look into their financial histories. Nicholson made money on the burst and... so did Warren. Their two friends, however, lost big time. How does that happen? One for all and all for one, right?"

He nodded. "But not in this case. What are you thinking?"

"I'm thinking insider trading. I couldn't figure out how Nicholson could have been savvy enough to see it coming—from what his mother told me, he wasn't that good at what he did—but if he somehow got the word and then passed it on to Warren...."

"*And*," Charlie said excitedly, "if he did, and if he didn't pass the word to his other two friends, Myers and Harrison—I wonder just how friendly they all were." He shook his head. "If he didn't let them in on it, and they lost big, they'd be really pissed, especially if they found out that Nicholson and Warren made out like bandits. That alone would be more than enough motive, right?"

"If they knew about it, yes, which makes the answer to your question... significant. But here's another question: Why didn't he include them? You're right; just how friendly were they all, I wonder.... No, Charlie. He had to have known something, and he must have told Warren, but not the other two."

"Are you thinking what I'm thinking?"

"Yeah. We may just have stumbled on the answer; that's what Nicholson had on Warren. Hell, if it got out that Warren had been insider trading, not only would it have ruined him, insider trading is federal. He would have gone to jail for at least a couple of years, maybe more. That by itself would have been motive enough for him to kill Nicholson, let alone the loss of the love of his life."

Charlie nodded, got to his feet, tipped up his cup and poured the dregs of the now cold decaf down his throat and said, "I need to do a little more digging. See what I can find out."

"Sounds like a plan," I said. "I'll have Ronnie dig a little more too. Let me know if you find anything. In the meantime...."

"Yeah, don't call me, I'll call you, right?"

"Something like that. See ya, Charlie."

After he'd gone I called Ronnie into my office and asked him to dig deeper into the investment histories of Warren, Harrison, and Myers and, as an afterthought, into Peter Nicholson's investments and who his friends in the world of finance had been.

"Go all the way back to 1997," I told him.

"What am I supposed to be looking for?"

"Anything out of the ordinary." I didn't tell him I was looking for evidence of insider trading. Ronnie can get a little one-track minded, so I try to give him as much latitude as I can; if Nicholson and Warren had been up to any monkey business, Ronnie would find it.

That done, I called Helen Nicholson and arranged to take her to lunch two days later, on Wednesday. I tried for Tuesday but she had a prior commitment. At first I was a bit bothered about the delay, but of course there was no hurry. The case was fifteen years cold, and nobody was going anywhere. I had all the time in the world. And I had to wait: for DNA results, for the court hearing.... *Aw hell. I'm going home.*

Except I couldn't. It was only ten thirty in the morning. I sighed, straightened my computer screen, adjusted the position of the keyboard, then the mouse, then I picked up the phone and called Kate.

"You've reached Lieutenant Gazzara, Major Cri...."

I hung up without leaving a message, flopped back in my chair, stared up at the chandelier. *I'll call Dad... nope, he's in court today.*

I stared around the room, spotted my shoulder rig and PV9 hanging on the coatrack. *That's it. I need some range time.... Maybe Amanda'd like to come with me.*

I called her.

"Hello. This is Amanda Starke, please leave me a...."

I guess I'll go by myself, then.

And I did; I blew through two hundred rounds at Shooter's Depot, banging them all over the place, and was glad I'd come alone. I was rusty as hell. I hadn't shot for more than two months—before the honeymoon I'd made it a habit to practice at least once a week—and it showed. Toward the end, however, with a little extra concentration, it was beginning to come back and, by the end of the session the six-inch pattern had shrunk to a more respectable two inches. I could live with that.

21

WEDNESDAY, JANUARY 18, 9:00 A.M

I didn't bother to go into work on Tuesday. Instead, I met my father and Rose for lunch and then played nine holes, by myself, in the afternoon—have you ever played golf by yourself? It was freezing cold, and the most boring two hours of my life. Even the pro thought I'd gone nuts when I told him what I was about to do, and managed to come up with some half-assed excuse why he couldn't go out with me. I was tempted to ask him for a lesson, get him out of his nice warm shop, but hell, I was in no mood to have my game chopped all to hell by a vengeful teacher, so I went out and played against myself —two balls, one against the other and, surprise, surprise: I won.

Jeez, I have to dig myself out of this rut somehow.

Tuesday evening went a whole lot better. Amanda arrived home early from work—she wasn't yet officially on board at Channel 7, but she couldn't stay away from the place—and we had a nice quiet evening at home together. I really was beginning to like this married-life thing.

And then Wednesday arrived, and had I known in advance what would happen, I wouldn't have gone in that day either.

Even from the beginning, the omens did not bode well. The mountain was again shrouded in icy fog, and to make matters worse the temperature was also below freezing. Amanda decided to stay home and enjoy a quiet day, and she tried to persuade me to do likewise, but I was in one of those antsy moods where I couldn't stay still for more than a few minutes. I needed to be working, or at least *at* work. True, I had a lunch appointment with Helen Nicholson at noon, but I decided to brave the elements and headed down Scenic Highway, through the fog and icy mist, and with a sigh of relief, rolled out onto Cummings Highway at the bottom of the mountain. I didn't get in until just after nine.

"Anything for me?" I asked as I pushed through the side door, stripping off my gloves and jacket.

Jacque looked up, shaking her head. "No. Everything is ticking right along. Bob has a handle on just about everything."

Sheesh. I might have to buy that boat after all. I'm sure as hell not needed here.

"I turned on your logs," she said. "You can grab a coffee and go put your feet up for a while."

It would have been easy to take that the wrong way, but I could see she was smiling as she said it, and I knew it was all part and parcel of her personality. So I did as she suggested. Twenty minutes later, I'd had enough and was ready to make someone's life hell.

I went into the outer office, looked around, spotted Ronnie leafing through a pile of papers, and decided it was to be him.

I walked quietly up behind him. "What did you did you find? Anything?"

He almost jumped out of his skin. "Damn! You startled me. No. Well... not much."

My heart sank. If Ronnie hadn't found anything, there was nothing to find.

"Not much? What's 'not much'?"

"Well, as you know," he said, reaching for his mouse and bringing up a page of dates and numbers I couldn't make heads or tails of, "all four of them were heavily invested in startup companies—IPOs—during the dot-com bubble. Webvan.com and Pets.com being just two of the biggest. During that five-year period, Nicholson cleaned up, made close to a quarter-million dollars. The other three didn't do too bad either. They all made a little money. Warren was up about $10,000 when the bubble burst; the other two a little less than that. Myers had almost $100,000 invested, most of it borrowed. Harrison had almost $115,000—again, almost all of it borrowed money.

"Just before the collapse of Pets.com in November of 2000, Nicholson shorted all his stock. Over the next several weeks, he made almost $25,000. His three friends lost everything they'd invested in that particular outfit.

Webvan tumbled in July and, guess what?" He looked up at me.

"He did it again?"

"Yup. Three weeks before the crash, he unloaded his stock, *and so did Warren*. Myers and Harrison, however, stayed in the game, and again they lost everything; Nicholson and Warren cleaned up."

"Okay, so that just confirms what we already knew."

"Yeah, but what's new is—and it's just conjecture, Mr. Starke, but—Nicholson's timing was impeccable. There was talk that he was about to be investigated by the SEC when he died. It looks greasy. I'm almost certain Nicholson knew somebody in the know. For five years he went through the motions, barely making a living, and then all that changed. Not only was he able to get in at the beginning of a good run, he also seems to have had an uncanny ability to read the trends. But if it really was his ability to read the markets, he would have been a whole lot more wealthy than he was. His picks were sporadic, and unlikely, but his timing was... well, as I said, impeccable. Suspicious, to say the least."

"So. Insider trading."

He nodded. "Had to be."

"What about Warren? Was he playing the same game?"

"No, I don't think so, at least not until Webvan. He was, I think, riding Nicholson's coattails. Nicholson was probably feeding them tips, which in itself is not unusual... unless those tips are coming from someone in the know, on the inside. On the buy side, they were all within an hour or two of one another. You could say they were just acting on educated advice, I suppose. On the sell side, no! Only Warren seemed privy to that information, and then only for the Webvan deal."

"Your conclusions, then?" I asked.

He shrugged. "Insider trading, but there's no way to prove it now. We can look at the big picture and be certain what was going on, but that's it. Sorry, boss."

I nodded and left him to it, the wheels in my head spinning.

It was maybe five minutes later that my cell phone rang.

"Hey, Kate," I said. "What's the haps?"

"You better sit down, Harry. I have some bad news for you."

"I *am* sitting down. What's wrong?"

"It's your client, Helen Nicholson. She's dead. Less than an hour ago."

22

WEDNESDAY, JANUARY 18, 10:00 A.M

I was struck dumb. My head spun. All kinds of thoughts flashed through my mind.

"Where, for God's sake? How?"

"Hit and run. No, not that. This was cold blooded, really cold blooded. She'd been to her yoga class at Warehouse Row and was in the parking garage, on the second floor. Someone in a pickup truck ran her down, *backed up over her*, then drove off. She died in the ambulance on the way to Erlanger."

My blood began to boil. I clamped my eyes shut, so tightly that I could see white lights flashing in the darkness. I opened them, shook my head.

"Did they catch him?" I asked quietly. I was hoping they had, and that Kate might give me five minutes with him—no two would be more than enough.

"Nope. There were two witnesses, though: a doctor who was going back to his car, who was maybe twenty feet away when it happened. And a mother with a young daughter, who was about to back her car out of her spot. Neither of them got a good look at the driver. Both of them agreed he was wearing a dark-colored hoodie. The EMTs did what they could for her but... well, her chest was crushed. She was never going to make it."

"How about the truck? Either of the witnesses get a plate number?"

"Yep. The doc got everything but the last digit. It was a Dodge 2500 diesel reported stolen last night, and found abandoned on the ground floor of the same garage, the engine still running. Whoever it was had a switch car right there in the garage."

"Security cameras?

"Nuh uh. Nothing."

"Where's the truck now?"

"On its way to Mike Willis."

"I'm on my way. Meet me there, okay?"

"Wait, don't hang up."

"What?"

"It's my case, Harry, not yours."

"So?"

I heard her sigh. "Yeah, so. What the hell. Okay, I'll meet you there. They'll be expecting you."

SHE WAS WAITING for me inside the compound when I arrived. I pulled up at the gate, waited for it to roll open, and then drove inside and parked.

"You're not going to like this," Kate said as we walked

across the lot to the shop. "She took a hell of a hit before she was crushed."

The truck, now inside a perimeter of black-and-yellow tape, was a brute, a lifted Dodge Ram 2500 Outdoorsman 4x4. It was big, black, and sported a custom front bumper that incorporated a bull bar and a winch. And the truck, a 2016 model, looked to be almost brand new; as far as I could see there wasn't a mark on it... other than the blood and flesh in and around the winch housing. Kate was right; Helen had taken one hell of a hit, and not just from the winch. That would have hit just above the knees; the bull bar was eighteen inches higher and would have hit her right in the gut.

She must have been as good as dead even before he hit her again.

Willis and another tech, both dressed from head to toe in white Tyvek, were already at work. He looked up through the windshield.

"Hey, Harry," he said as he backed out of the cab. "This is a bad one, huh?" He pulled off the latex gloves and offered me his hand.

"This is a show truck—" he turned and looked at it admiringly "—but the bed's trashed, loaded with 8 × 8 × 16 concrete construction blocks, almost a ton of 'em, I should guess, just thrown in there. The guy who owns this truck will pitch a fit when he gets it back. I doubt he would ever have allowed so much as a cardboard box in the bed. Whoever loaded it did it for the extra weight. They loaded it to kill, no doubt about it. That's what you call 'premeditated,' Harry."

"Any chance we could trace the supplier?" Kate asked.

"Of the blocks? It's not likely. I doubt they got 'em from the local Lowes. They could have come from any one of fifty builder's yards in the area; probably stolen, like the truck."

Kate nodded. "Anything inside the cab?"

"Uh.... *I don't know,*" he said sarcastically. "I've only had the thing a few minutes. Ask me in a couple of hours. Maybe I'll have something for you then."

I walked slowly around the taped perimeter. I made a full circle, ending up back at the front. I stared down at the winch, at the heavy hook wound tightly into the housing. It stuck out maybe four or five inches and I could see, even without touching it, that it was immovable; it was also covered in blood and tissue. I shuddered to think of the wound it must have inflicted.

No, I don't want to know. Not this time. I'd like to remember her as the beautiful woman she was. Not the broken, bloody....

"Hey, Harry. You still with us?"

I looked up. Kate had her hands stuck in her back pockets; her head was tilted, the look questioning.

I heaved a sigh. "Yeah. I'm still with you."

I rejoined the group, now grown to six. Willis was pulling out all the stops. Good.

"Come on, Harry," Kate said. "We need to talk. I'll buy you lunch, okay?"

"That will be a first," I joked, but there was no humor

in my voice. "The Boathouse is just down the road. That work for you?"

"It will. My car or yours?"

"Mine, of course. I had enough riding in cruisers ten years ago."

She smiled. "C'mon then. There's nothing we can do here."

THE BOATHOUSE IS KIND OF unique. It sits just off Amnicola on the banks of the Tennessee River. On a nice day, a meal there is a pleasant experience. The food is good, and the view stunning.

That day, however, was not nice. The icy rain was whipped by a fifteen-knot wind and the river had white-caps on it. It was a day not unlike the night now more than two years ago when Tabitha Willard decided to throw herself off the Walnut Street Bridge. Those weren't good memories either, though, and by the time we found a table and were seated, I was in a terrible mood.

One of these days, I'm gonna have to quit this stupid life. I don't know how much more death and heartache I can stand. No wonder Richard quit and became a barber. I mean, jeez. I stared out of the window at the rain and the turbulent waters of the Tennessee. *I came back from the best six weeks of my life to this. A kind and lovely lady smashed down in a goddamn parking garage, for God's sake... and the weather sucks; it really sucks.*

"Harry? *Harry?*"

I came back to earth with a bump. "Yeah? What?"

"Where the hell were you? I've been talking to you; you haven't heard a word I've said."

"Yeah. Sorry. I was feeling sorry for myself, is all.... What were you saying?"

"I was saying... no, I was asking, if you thought this is tied into your investigation."

"What the hell do you think? Of course it is. Somebody thinks that with Helen Nicholson out of the way, I'll quit. No friggin' chance of that, though."

I stared across the table at her. She stared back. "What?" I asked.

"You know what. I want it, and I want it all."

I sighed and shook my head. Yes, I did know. I'd been expecting it.

"I'll have Tim make copies of everything relevant." I took out my iPhone, hit the speed dial for my office, told Jacque what I needed Tim to do, and asked her to get everything over to Kate's office as soon as possible.

"Happy?" I asked, as I slid the phone back into my jacket pocket.

She didn't answer immediately, but then, "I don't know, Harry. 'Happy' is not the word I would use, not even satisfied. I know you. I know what you're thinking, and I don't like it. If you're going to work with me—"

"Whoa!" I said it a whole lot louder than I intended to, and attracted a lot of alarmed and annoyed looks from the patrons scattered around us.

"That's not the way I see it," I said. "I'm not working

with *you*. You can work with *me*, if you want, but this is my case and, and, and... it's my case. You can work it with me or you can work it on your own; your choice."

She folded her arms across her chest, and no, she wasn't happy, not at all, but I wasn't about to soften my position. Except then I did just that.

"Let's work together, okay? A partnership. That's it. Take it or leave it."

For a long time, she didn't move or say anything, and then she simply nodded and unfolded her arms.

We ate lunch in silence and then ordered coffee. I just wasn't in the mood for conversation.

"Snap out of it, Harry," she said suddenly. "This is not like you."

I looked at her, put my cup down, and said, "Yeah, it is. Over the past few years I've known a lot of good people that died too soon. Kate, I mean, I never really got over Tabitha Willard. The look she gave me that night she jumped off the bridge... I still dream about it. And Charlie Maxwell, what about her? You didn't know her, but she was a beautiful person, inside and out. And Emily, the chief's daughter. You knew her. What a sweetheart she was. And... and... now Helen Nicholson. Kate.... Aw hell. What's the point?"

"It's the job, Harry. It's what we do. It's what we *choose* to do. You told me that a long time ago. Remember?"

I nodded. She was right. I looked at her and, for a moment, I remembered the day now more than sixteen years ago when they'd foisted a fresh-faced, naive kid on me as my new partner. I wasn't happy about it then, but it turned out to be one of the best things that ever happened to me.

"Yep, you're right. You wanted to talk, so talk."

"As I said: I know you, Harry. You've been working this case for what, ten days?"

"Nine."

"Okay, nine. You must have some ideas, right? I'd like to know what you're thinking."

"You're wrong, Kate. I don't. I know who I like for it —Ellis Warren—but liking him for it and being able to prove it are two different things. Look. Let's do it this way: you go back to the station. Take a look at the stuff I had Tim put together for you, and then we'll get together tomorrow and go over it. Maybe between us we can come up with something. There's not much else we can do until we get Peter Nicholson's body exhumed and I get the DNA back. We also need to know what Willis will find in the truck, if anything. You can get that from him later today. In the meantime, I'm going home to Amanda, a warm fire, and a half bottle of Laphroaig. My office at nine in the morning. That good for you?"

It was, and that was how we left it.

23

THURSDAY, JANUARY 19, 9:00 A.M

Thursday, January 19, 9:00 a.m.
The weather had not improved. If anything, when I woke up the next morning, it had gotten worse. The Southeastern United States is a beautiful place to live, except in winter. That Thursday morning the temperature had risen to a balmy forty-three degrees, and the rain was coming down hard, the way it had been doing all night long. I, that is we, woke early to find a thunderstorm raging around us. Lighting lit up our bedroom, so bright I swear I could see Amanda's bones. It didn't last long; the thunder and lightning were gone by six o'clock, and although the storm wasn't over—still a deluge—it was a lot less violent. Even so, Amanda was on edge, and I have to admit, I was a little shaken myself.

And so I missed my early morning run yet again, and I would have stayed home again too if I hadn't arranged to meet Kate at nine that morning. So, three cups of coffee, a waffle, and a fried egg later, I headed down the mountain through the wind and the rain and the fog. Oh how I missed those balmy days on Calypso Key.

Thirty minutes later I was happily settled behind my desk in my second-favorite place on earth. Kate arrived a few minutes later.

"Hey," I said as she came in. "Did Mike Willis find anything?"

"For God's sake, Harry. Let me get through the door, will you?"

"Yeah, sit down, sit down…. Well, did he?"

She sighed, set her coffee on my desk, and said, "Yes. He found three hairs on the driver's seat and headrest. Dark hairs. Helen is blonde, so they're not hers. I had him send them to the lab for DNA testing. I've also had him send a tech to the owner for a sample. The hairs could be his, so we need to be able to eliminate him. There was nothing else. No prints. Mike thought there might have been something on the cab floor—it's been wet outside for days—but there wasn't. Those three hairs are it, and without a suspect to match them to…."

"Oh, we have suspects. What we don't have is their DNA, and how the hell we're going to get it I have no idea."

She nodded. "So why don't you take me through it? Might as well begin at the beginning."

The box of evidence was still on my desk. I asked her to grab it and take it into the conference room where I had my board set up. Then I made myself coffee and joined her there. We spent the next two hours going over everything. When we were done, she leaned back in her chair, looked at me thoughtfully, and said, "You really don't have a damned thing, do you? Harry, it could be any one of those three," she said, and waved a hand at the suspects on the board. "There's no way, with what you have here, that you can pin Peter Nicholson's death on any of them—or all of them. They, he, whoever, got away with it. It's done. Over."

I stared back at her.

Damn it. She's right. "If we get permission to exhume him, all we'll get out of it is a change of cause of death. But I promised Helen I'd find her son's killer and, one way or another, that's what I intend to do."

"One way or another? Harry...."

I shrugged. "Look, I think it was Helen's request for an exhumation order that was the direct cause of her death. If that's true, one of those three—" I pointed toward the board "—killed her. The question is why he, whichever one it is, doesn't want Peter dug up."

"And you think you know, right?"

"No, I don't know," I said, frustrated by the question. "Not for sure. You've looked at the photos, the videos, the autopsy report. He died of a single shotgun blast to the chest. Even if we exhume the body, what's to find?"

I paused, thought for a moment, then continued, "Right now, whoever it was who killed Helen is thinking he's covered his tracks, that the exhumation can't go forward, but I'll rope in Steve Walker and Doc Sheddon. Law enforcement and the medical examiner have the authority to independently request a body be exhumed if there's a compelling reason to do it, and a botched first autopsy and a doubtful cause of death are, in my opinion, damned good reasons."

She nodded. "Good luck with that. Unfortunately, my only interest in your cold case is the impact it has on my investigation.... I need DNA samples from the three amigos up there to compare with the hairs Willis found in the truck." She turned and stared at the photographs of Warren, Myers, and Harrison. "But we're not going to get a court order using a fifteen-year-old closed case as leverage."

"And we sure as hell can't just go ask them," I said, thinking out loud. "Hmmm. They're all members of the club. Warren shouldn't be too difficult. He plays golf with August now and then. The other two... I don't know. It might be a long wait, but I have all the time in the world."

"Hah," she growled. "You might, but I don't. I have the chief breathing down my neck. Helen Nicholson was friends with his wife."

"Well, there's not a whole lot we can do right now. It's going to take four or five weeks until Willis gets the results on the hairs back from the lab. In the meantime, I'll see what I can do about obtaining DNA samples from the suspects."

"That's it? That's all you have to offer?"

"Unless you can come up with something else, yeah."

"Wow, Sherlock. You must be losing it."

I grinned at her. "Maybe, maybe not. We'll see. You want to attend the exhumation hearing with me next week?"

"Sure. Why not. You wanna come to Helen Nicholson's post tomorrow morning? Doc's scheduled it for nine."

"Not only no, but hell no. Give me a call when it's done, though."

She nodded. "Well, it's time I got back to the department. I want to go through all that crap you left me again. Maybe I'll find something you missed." She smiled as she said it.

I smiled back. "Yeah? That would be a first."

"Not hardly," she said, closing the door behind her, leaving me staring up at the three enigmatic faces on the board. I could have sworn they were mocking me.

24

WEDNESDAY FEBRUARY 1, 9:00 A.M

The next few days dragged by in much the same vein as the ten that had gone before. There were no new revelations, either about the Peter Nicholson case or his mother's. The weather didn't improve and neither did my mood. I spent a long weekend brooding about both cases. I watched the videos until my eyes hurt, again without learning anything new.

Sunday came and my weekly round of golf with August and his buddies was canceled due to the incessant rain. We did, however, join them for lunch at the club. I would rather have stayed home, but I figured I might be able to grab some DNA. The Warrens were always there, no matter the weather. This time, however, they were not. Still, lunch was good, and we always enjoy spending time with my old man—and Rose, bless her. She's a trip.

I didn't hear anything from Kate either, not until the Tuesday afternoon before the hearing, and then only to confirm that she would be attending. We agreed to meet at my office and walk to the courthouse together.

And that Wednesday morning, the weather changed. I woke to a clear sky full of stars, and I felt good. Was it an omen of good things to come? I hoped to hell it was.

JUDGE HARRIS PEERED over the top of his glasses at my father and said, "Mr. Starke. You are petitioning the court for permission to exhume the body of one Peter Nicholson, and you are doing so namely on behalf of the decedent's mother, Mrs. Helen Nicholson, the Hamilton County Sheriff's Department, and the Hamilton County Medical Examiner. Is that correct?"

"It is, Your Honor."

"But it's my understanding that Mrs. Nicholson is herself now deceased, and that the decedent's next of kin..." he looked at his notes "...Mrs. Mary Ann Warren, does not wish the body of her late husband to be disinterred. Is that also correct?"

"It is."

"Then I fail to understand why we're here," Harris said, leaning back in his chair. "Please explain, sir."

"Your Honor," August said, "Peter Nicholson's death is highly suspicious and its cause as recorded by the medical examiner at the time is not supported by the results of the somewhat limited autopsy performed at the time of his death. The co-petitioners argue that the interests of justice require an exhumation and a full and proper postmortem examination."

It was at this point that John Dooley, the Warren's attorney, rose to his feet and said, "If I may, Your Honor?"

The judge peered over his glasses at him and then at August, who nodded.

"You may, Mr. Dooley."

"Your Honor, my client—" he turned slightly toward Mary Ann, who was seated next to him, and it was just her; Ellis Warren wasn't present "—the deceased's ex-wife and next of kin strongly opposes the proposed course of action. Her husband was the victim of a horrendous accident, as was established at the time of his death, and she maintains that it would be an egregious act of disrespect to, and I quote her own words, 'dig him up after all this time.' Therefore, Your Honor, I respectfully request that you dismiss the petition and let her late husband rest in peace. Thank you."

Again, Harris consulted his notes. "We'll see, Mr. Dooley. Mr. Starke," he continued. "The cause of death as listed on both the death certificate and the autopsy report is accidental. The decedent tripped and fell on his shotgun. The gun went off and he died as a result of the wound he received. Am I to understand that the petitioners are disputing the cause of death?"

"They are, Your Honor. It is our contention that the initial autopsy was incomplete, flawed, and that a second autopsy could establish that the cause of death was not an accident, but homicide. We believe that a second forensic examination of the wound is needed to pinpoint the exact type of weapon and how it was used to inflict the killing shot. We further contend that Peter Nicholson did not fall on his gun, but was shot to death by a person or persons as yet unknown, and we have discovered new evidence to support that belief."

"Yes, so I understand...." He thought for a moment and then continued, "Mr. Starke, I'm not in favor of disinterment. Public policy is that the sanctity of the grave should be maintained and that, once buried, a body should not be disturbed. Courts, this one included, do not order or permit a body to be disinterred except in extraordinary circumstances, where the court can be persuaded that disinterment would further the interests of justice. But the need for an autopsy might be one such circumstance. My reading of the law states that courts may permit a body to be exhumed and an autopsy to be performed in order to discover truth and promote justice. So, Mr. Starke. If I am to grant an order of disinterment for the purpose of such an examination, good cause and exigent circumstances must exist. That appears to be what we have in this case, but...."

He looked at Mary Ann Warren and her lawyer. "Mr. Dooley. Can you give me a good reason why I should not grant the petition?"

Dooley rose to his feet. "I can, Your Honor. My client strongly objects to her late husband's remains being disturbed on the whim of a distraught mother who happens herself to no longer be living. Furthermore, the cause of death was clearly defined at the time by both the medical examiner and the Hamilton County sheriff as an accident. The petitioners cite new evidence, but as far as I can see, there is *nothing* new. They, Sheriff Walker, Dr. Sheddon, and..." he looked around at me and shook his head as if in disbelief "...and the private investigator Mr. Starke, have simply trotted out what was already available to the authorities at the time of Peter Nicholson's death and have offered nothing more than a different interpretation of it; an entirely subjective interpretation, I might add, and one not borne out by the facts. I therefore repeat my request that you dismiss the petition and allow poor Mr. Nicholson to remain at rest and in peace."

"Yes," Harris said, dryly, as he looked over his glasses at me. "I've seen the evidence, and I do agree there are some anomalies. In fact, it appears to me that the 2002 investigation of the incident was somewhat... sloppy, shall we say? Even so, I'm not sure you've met the requirements: good cause and exigent circumstances. I'm still of the opinion that there may not be enough here to support such a drastic step as disinterment." He looked at my father. "Mr. Starke?"

"Your Honor," August said, "I understand your concern and believe I can show both good cause and exigent circumstances. I'd like to call upon Mr. Harry Starke to offer an explanation of the petitioners' interpretation of the evidence and his opinion as to the cause of Mr. Nicholson's death."

Harris looked at Dooley. "Any objection?"

I suppose Dooley must have realized that there was no point in objecting to my giving evidence, because he didn't. He did, however object to my offering an opinion as to the cause of death, stating that only a qualified medical doctor could do that.

"My apologies, Your Honor. Mr. Starke will not be offering an opinion as to the *cause* of death, merely the *manner* of death. As a homicide detective of more than sixteen years, he more than qualifies as an expert witness and as such will testify that the evidence—the original evidence—shows that the *manner* of death was not an accident but a homicide."

I thought that Dooley was going to object to the use of the semantics. In fact, he half stood and opened his mouth to do so, but changed his mind and sat down again.

Anyway, Harris agreed with August and I was duly sworn in. I was then asked to identify myself for the record. That done, August asked me to explain my interpretation of the evidence.

"Mr. Starke. You were hired by Mrs. Helen Nicholson to investigate the death of her son, which occurred while he was out hunting in Prentice Cooper State Forest on Friday May 3, 2002. Is that correct?"

"Yes."

"And during your investigation, were you afforded the opportunity to study the evidence retrieved by the sheriff's department and the reports generated by the detectives from that department and from the medical examiner's office?"

"I was."

August nodded. "I understand, Mr. Starke, that your

studies caused you to have doubts as to the true cause of Mr. Nicholson's death. Is that also correct?"

"It is."

"In that case, I'd like you to explain your findings to the court." And he sat down.

Now you should understand that I, that is, we didn't want to provide the Warrens and their attorneys with everything we had. My job was to provide the judge with just enough to persuade him to grant the petition. I had a plan which I hoped would do just that, but I was prepared to go further, if I had to. I began by stating the basic reasons I believed that Peter's death was no accident. But having said that, I soon found that I had opened myself up not only to questioning, but to ridicule.

"So, Mr. Starke," Dooley said with a sarcastic smile. "That's quite a fantasy. You can read palms too, I bet."

"No."

"You have the second sight, then?"

It's been said that I do, but I'm not going to hand that one to you.

"No."

"Then you must have been there, in the forest, all those years ago," he said sarcastically.

"No."

"No. You weren't there. In fact, no one was there when Mr. Nicholson died, so how could you possibly know what happened?"

"Mr. Dooley. I beg to differ. Someone *was* there, as I have just explained in detail. Would you like me to go over it again so that even you can understand it?"

"That won't be necessary, Mr. Starke, thank you; I understand perfectly well. You say that it's impossible for the body of Peter Nicholson to have landed on top of the gun as shown in this photograph?" He handed it to me. I recognized it as a copy of one that I'd gotten from Sheriff Walker.

"That's correct. It would not be possible."

"What if I told you I could produce an expert witness that would testify that it's entirely possible for it to have happened that way?"

I shrugged. "Then that person would not be an expert, and I could produce at least half a dozen more experts that would support the impossibility of what you see in this photograph.... Mr. Dooley. Have you ever fired a 12-gauge shotgun?"

"You are here to answer questions, Mr. Starke, not—"

"No, no," Harris said, resting his chin on his clenched fists. "I'd like to know the answer. Have you ever fired such a shotgun, Mr. Dooley?"

"No, Your Honor, I have not."

Harris nodded. "I thought not. Make your point, Mr. Starke."

"It involves one of the basic laws of physics, Your Honor. I'm sure you've heard of it: Newton's Third Law. It states that for every action there is an equal and opposite reaction."

Judge Harris nodded. "And it applies in this case?"

"It does. When a bullet is fired from a gun, the *force* of the internal explosion pushes the bullet forward as a projectile. This is an action. The sudden recoil of the gun caused by that same internal explosion is the *equal and opposite* force applied by the explosion to the bullet. But a .22 would have little recoil when compared to a .45. In this case, however, we have a 12-gauge shotgun which produced, by comparison even to a .45, a massive internal explosion against more than an ounce of lead." I looked up at the judge; he nodded.

"The reason I asked Mr. Dooley if he'd ever fired a shotgun was because if he had, he would have known that the gun in this case could not possibly have ended up where it did, cuddled closely beneath Peter Nicholson's chest. If he'd ever fired such a gun he would remember the tremendous violence of the recoil. He would also know that if such a gun is not held tightly to the shoulder, the recoil could, and probably would, inflict serious injury to the gunner. Your Honor, such haphazard handling of such a weapon has been known to break, even shatter, the clavicle."

Again the judge nodded, but now he was staring at Dooley, and I'm sure he knew what was coming next.

"So," I continued. "We know that he had to have been holding it loosely, in one hand, probably his right hand, but here's where things get a little tricky. There's no possible way that gun could have fired by accident, not unless he was carrying it with his finger on the trigger, and *no one*, not even a *rookie*, ever does that. It's dangerous, and a gun that size is just too heavy." I paused and looked out at the faces. There wasn't a smile among them.

"But let's say—" and I smiled as I continued "—just for argument's sake, that he was indeed carrying his gun with his finger on the trigger, and that he had inadvertently pulled the trigger and fired the gun.... Where do you suppose the gun would have been aimed? Not at his damned chest, that's for certain. And then we have to consider that pesky Third Law. Even if he'd been a contortionist and somehow managed to point the thing at his chest, the recoil would have sent it spiraling into the air.... It would have landed perhaps a dozen feet from the body, not underneath it. No.... Someone else was holding the gun, or a gun; someone else pulled the trigger; someone else killed him; and someone else staged the scene to make it look like an accident."

The courtroom was silent, and then Judge Harris asked quietly, "Suppose he dropped the gun. Could it have gone off accidentally when the butt hit the ground?"

"No, Your Honor. That's not possible. I myself have done extensive research and this particular brand has been deemed to be one of the safest guns available. Not only that, I have it on good authority that Peter Nicholson was properly trained in the use of firearms of all types and was very safety conscious; he habitually carried his shotgun with the breach open."

"I've heard enough." Harris banged his gavel. "Petition granted."

"I HAVE a feeling we'd better get this done as quickly as possible," August said to Doc Sheddon as we stood together in the lobby outside the courtroom. "I have no doubt Dooley will appeal the decision on Mrs. Warren's behalf."

"I agree," Sheddon said, "and I'll get right on it. Give me five minutes; I'll make a couple of calls." He reached inside his coat, took his cell phone from his pocket, and turned and walked a few steps along the corridor.

"It's all set," he said when he returned. "Tomorrow morning at five o'clock. I intend to be there. How about you, Harry? Kate?"

Kate nodded. "Might be interesting."

I nodded, and said, "Of course. Is there anything I can do?"

"No," Sheddon said. "I've arranged for lights and a machine and a small flatbed truck to be at the cemetery at 5:00 a.m. I understand he was buried in one of those concrete vaults. It shouldn't take long to get him out of the ground.... but that vault is a bit of a problem. It won't fit through the doors at my lab, so we'll have to use the motor pool's forklift to get the thing off the truck bed. We'll open it there. The casket itself will fit in the back of my Suburban. It's just a few hundred yards from there to my lab. I'll try to get through it all before we get served with a restraining order."

"Fine," I said. "I'll see you at five."

"That's it then," he said. "I'm heading home to get some rest. Tomorrow with be a busy day. Have a good night everyone."

25

THURSDAY, FEBRUARY 2, 5:00 A.M

W hen I drove through the gates of Lakeshore Memorial Gardens the following morning it was just a couple of minutes after five o'clock, and the weather had turned nasty yet again. It was raining steadily, a black and dismal morning, and again I wondered if the omens were against us.

Doc was already at the gravesite when I got there, standing under an umbrella. How long he'd been there, I didn't know, nor did I ask. I could tell he was in no mood to chat. He simply nodded at me and turned again to watch the men working just a few yards away.

A generator was running quietly, four sets of lights on poles were in place, and a backhoe was growling away, already clearing the sod from the grave.

Doc was right. It didn't take long. The grave was quickly opened and two sets of chains were attached to the backhoe's bucket. Minutes later, the concrete vault containing the casket and body of Peter Nicholson was deposited on the truck bed. From Lakeshore they took it to the motor pool on Amnicola, where they removed the vault from the truck, the casket from the vault, and slid it into the back of Doc's SUV, which he drove two blocks to the Hamilton County Forensic Center.

By eight o'clock that morning he had opened the casket and was ready to begin work. Those present to witness the procedure included me, of course; Carol Owens, the Center's forensic anthropologist; Kate; Sheriff Walker; and... Thomas Dooley Esq., attorney for Ellis and Mary Ann Warren.

I peered over the rim of the casket. *Woah.* I was startled to see a well-preserved body, not the decayed corpse I was expecting. The cheeks were hollowed, the mouth open, the skin stretched tightly over the bones of the hands, but other than that he might well have been interred only a couple of weeks ago, rather than the fifteen years it actually was.

The body was lifted gently from the casket and laid on the autopsy table. Its clothes were removed. Carol slipped the wedding band off the third finger of his left hand and handed it to Dooley for safekeeping.

Doc then bent over the body and began to examine the wound.

"The entry wound is elliptical, indicating that the shot was fired from left to right at a sharply downward angle. The shot entered to the left of the sternum and appears to have traveled downward through the left lung and the heart. I'll be able to tell you for sure when I open the chest cavity." He reached for a set of metal calipers.

"The hole measures one inch in width, and...."

And so it went. At one point Kate left and came back with a Twix bar from the vending machine. I stayed the whole way through.

Four hours later, Sheddon had found five more number four pellets in the rear of Peter's chest cavity and come to the conclusion that the death had indeed been a homicide. He gratefully accepted the coffee Carol handed to him, and took a step back from the autopsy table.

We said nothing. He gets around to telling his story in his own good time, so we let him stand, sip his coffee, and stare down at the body. Finally, he set the cup down and began.

"He was leaning slightly forward when he was shot. The shot entered the body above and to the left of the sternum," he said, as he stepped up to the table and surveyed his handiwork. "It fragmented the third rib, passed though the apex of the left lung, and the heart. Death would have been virtually instantaneous." He stood with his arms folded, his chin on his chest, staring down over his glasses at the open cavity.

"And the rest of it is like I told Harry based on those photographs. No gunpowder residue or burn marks on the skin, and the scalloping indicates that the pellets had already begun to spread when they entered the chest. Based on the extent of the scalloping, I say that the shot was fired from between three to five feet away.

"Furthermore, when we examined the clothing he wore that day, we found nothing to indicate that the victim fell on his weapon. What blood there is on the gun was transferred after death, most likely when it was placed under the body.

"The angle and position of the wound indicates to me that he was either seated or crouched down when the load passed through his clothes and chest."

He sighed, then said, "Someone went to a great deal of trouble to stage the scene to make his death look like an accident."

He sipped his coffee, looked around at our silent faces. "So, people, what we have is an intermediate-to-distant range shotgun wound, not a contact or near-contact wound. Therefore, it is my intention to amend the death certificate. The cause of death is homicide."

I looked across the remains of Peter Nicholson at John Dooley. His face was a mask, expressionless, but it was obvious he wasn't happy with the verdict. Inwardly, I smiled. Outwardly, I was as solemn as he was. But then it hit me.

I already knew it wasn't an accident. I know no more now than I did when I walked in here four hours ago.

"Doc," I said. "I'm going to need a DNA sample. I was going to have Mrs. Nicholson supply it, but she's gone.... And a sample from the victim would be even better."

"I object to that, Dr. Sheddon," Dooley said. "Peter Nicholson's body has already been violated terribly by this... this *travesty*."

"Yes. His body sure as hell has been violated, but not by us," Doc said, fishing inside the chest cavity and extracting a small piece of tissue. "This should do it, I think." He held it up to the light. "Carol. Bag this for Harry, please."

Dooley glared at him. "Hurrrumpf!"

"I think we're done here," Sheddon said. "Tidy him up please, Carol. Let's get him back to Lakeshore where he belongs. Harry, Kate, Walker, is there anything else you need before we put him back to rest?"

I shook my head, as did the others.

"Good. You'll have my report by the end of the week. You too, Mr. Dooley," he added dryly. "Now, if you don't mind. It's been a long morning. I need coffee and food, and quickly. Anyone want to join me?"

No one did. I headed back to the office to get my sample off to DDC. Kate headed back to the department, Steve Walker to his office, and John Dooley.... Well, who the hell cared?

26

FRIDAY, FEBRUARY 3, 9:00 A.M

When I got in on Friday I shut myself in my office and spread everything out on my desk. The weekend was looming large in my thoughts, but not as large as the deaths of Peter and Helen Nicholson.

The DNA results for the blood on the wood chips and the samples taken from Peter Nicholson's shotgun had arrived on the nineteenth, the day after Helen died. The results for the chips were inconclusive; the samples were too degraded. The only thing they could say for sure was that the blood was human. Human? As evidence, that didn't mean a whole lot. We'd never know for sure if it was Peter's, but I was certain it was, especially when I read that the blood spatter on the gun *was* a match; it was his blood, and the only way it could have gotten there was for the gun to have been leaning against the stump when he was shot, just as I'd thought.

I was almost sure his killer and Helen's were the same

person, and I had a strong suspicion about who it was, but even when I had the DNA results from the hairs Mike Willis found in the truck, I couldn't prove a damn thing without something to compare it to.

I got up from my desk, wandered out into the bull pen, took note of what was going on, but it didn't register. I made coffee and went into the conference room, to the board with the photos of Dewey, Screwum, and Howe on it, and for a long moment I just stood there, staring at them. They, in turn, stared back at me. Were they smiling at me? Ellis Warren was, but the others....

Yeah. You are, you bastards. You're mocking me.

I took their abuse for a little while longer, and then I'd had enough. I turned away and, coffee in hand, returned to my own office and dumped myself despondently behind my desk.

I sorted through the photographs of the wound, both the old ones and those made during Doc Sheddon's second autopsy.

Okay. When you're stuck for answers, go back to basics, and first and most important of those is that every killer either leaves something at the scene or takes something away. So what have I missed?

I sorted through the box, and took each piece of evidence out and laid it on the desktop. I retrieved my magnifying glass from the desk drawer and, as I leafed through the photographs, I studied every inch of them, and then.... *Hmmm. I wonder. Hah!*

I sat back in the chair, magnifying glass in one hand, photo in the other. Finally I laid both down on the desk, kicked back, stared up at the chandelier, and smiled.

Which one is the most likely to talk to me, I wonder?

"HELLO. WHO IS THIS?"

"Hello, Heath. This is Harry Starke. I wondered if I could have a quick word."

"Starke? What the hell do you want? How did you get my private number?"

"Ah now, Heath. That would be telling. Let's just say I'm a detective, and leave it at that."

"You've got some nerve. What do you want? I don't have time to waste with you."

"I just have a couple of simple questions. Were you wearing a ball cap that day in Prentice Cooper?"

"What? Probably. Why?"

"What color was it?"

"How the hell should I know? It was fifteen years ago, for Christ's sake."

"Think about it, Heath. It's important. It could get you out of this mess."

I could almost hear the wheels turning inside his head. "I... I... green. It was a Packer's cap. I'm a fan... was a fan."

"You sure, Heath?"

"Yeah. I remember now. I had two of them. I wore one most of the time I wasn't at work. Hell, I think I still have one of them, somewhere. So, yes. I'm sure."

"How about Harrison? Was he wearing one?"

"Yeah. He'd just bought a John Deere lawn tractor. They were on sale and the dealer had thrown in the hat too, so it was brand new. He wouldn't shut up about that mower."

"Good. That's good, Heath. Now how about...."

"Warren? He was wearing a white one."

"White? You're sure?"

"Well, pretty sure. He liked white: golf jackets, golf gloves, hats, golf bag. He still does. You've seen him at the club; hell he even wears white pants these days."

"Okay. Final question, and this is the big one. What color cap was Peter Nicholson wearing?"

Silence. For several seconds he didn't speak, then, "He wasn't wearing one, I don't think. If he was, it would have been a first. He didn't like them. Said they messed up his hair."

I nodded to myself, smiling. "Thanks, Heath. I appreciate you taking the time."

"Are you going to tell me why you needed to know?"

"Not right now, but later. Listen. I may need to talk to you again. Would you mind?"

"Who are you trying to hang for this, Starke? It was an accident. I know; I found him."

"I'm not trying to hang anyone, Heath. I just want to find out what happened that day. So, can I call you or not?"

He was silent for a moment, then said, "Yeah. If it will help put an end to this mess, I suppose so." He sounded tired.

"Great. Thanks again."

I disconnected the call, leaned back in my chair, and stared at the photograph of Peter Nicholson's body lying facedown on the trail, the white ball cap lying nearby.

I need to call Kate. So that was what I did.

I hit the speed dial on my iPhone and waited, and waited, and then heard, "You've reached...."

Hell.

I waited until the greeting finished, and then, at the beep—*I hate that friggin' word*—I left her a message to call me as soon as she could. Then I called Mike Willis.

"Harry," he said, "you really are psychic. I was just about to call you. Can you come over?"

"You've got something for me?"

"Maybe. Twenty minutes, yeah?" He was smiling. I could tell.

"Yes, twenty. Listen. I just tried to call Kate, but had to leave her a message. Is she in the building, do you know?"

"I think so. I saw her about thirty minutes ago. You want me to have her join us?"

"If you wouldn't mind."

"Mind? Hah. It will be my pleasure."

"Good. See you in a few."

THEY WERE WAITING for me in the lobby of the Police Services Center.

"Let's go through to my office," Willis said. "I have something to show you that might be of interest."

His office was on the second floor of the building, and not much bigger than a closet. The shotgun and the bag of clothing I'd left with him were both on his desk. There wasn't really anywhere else to put them.

"Take a seat," he said, easing himself down into the worn office chair behind the desk. "I've asked Joanne Snyder to join us. She should be here any minute."

Barely had he finished the sentence than Joanne walked in, a small, somewhat elderly woman with graying hair and a pair of horn-rimmed glasses that made her look like a snowy owl. She also wore a white lab coat, open to reveal a white roll-neck sweater and dark gray pants. The ensemble completed the snowy owl look.

"Hey, Joanne. You know Harry Starke, right?"

"Oh yes. Hiya, Harry."

I got up from my seat and offered it to her. She refused, saying she preferred to stand.

"Okay, then. Let's get on with it," Willis said. He looked at Snyder. "You want to go first, or shall I?"

She shrugged. "Go ahead."

"Right. So, guys, I took a long hard look at the clothing; the gun, you already know about." He looked at me. I nodded.

"There are no powder burns on the vest, shirt, or undershirt around the hole. There is, however, high-velocity impact blood spatter—microscopic droplets, mist in the fibers of the cuffs and sleeves of Peter Nicholson's shirt, more on the left sleeve than on the right. The direction of travel is outward from the chest, indicating that the victim had his arms raised in a defensive posture like so." He raised his own arms to demonstrate and, with his right hand, indicated the inside of the left forearm. "Why it was not found during the first investigation I have no idea, but it should have been.

"And I'd be willing to bet," he continued, "that similar spatter was present on the backs of both hands, especially the left. There were also microscopic traces of grass stains on the knees of his pants. I think he may have been on his knees when he was killed."

"That's what you said last time I was here, and it fits with Doc Sheddon's findings," I said. "He said he thought Nicholson might have been crouched down when he was shot."

Willis nodded. "Right. Good. That makes sense. So let's talk about the blood spatter. High-velocity impact blood spatter, such as we have here, produced by an extremely powerful weapon, such as a 12-gauge shotgun, would travel perhaps five to ten feet from the source. It would be present as droplets, microscopic droplets, and mist. Spatter is present, as we already know, on the cuffs and sleeves of the victim's shirt and, as we discussed last time, it's on the weapon, but not where we'd expect it to be. That being so, we know this is not the weapon that killed him." He looked at me, then Kate, then back at me. We waited patiently for him to tell us.

Why is it that all these folks think they have to be showmen? Get on with it, man.

"Yes, Mike we know that, but you've found something else, right?"

He nodded, grinned, pulled on a pair of latex gloves, and reached into the bag. When his hand emerged it was holding the baggie that contained the white ball cap.

Damn! I knew it.

He took the cap from the baggie and held it in front of him, the fist of his right hand inside it.

"Two things," he said. "One, I found five hairs caught in the buckle and four more inside the cap itself; three with the follicles still intact. Second, there's high-velocity impact blood spatter present on the bill, here." He pointed with his left hand.

"Okay," I said. "I'd expect to find blood and hairs on and in the cap, which is why I called you. What's the problem?"

"Yes, and I would have expected it too, but here's the thing. The blood spatter is traveling in the wrong direction. It should be going from in to out, under the bill, but it's traveling from *out to in*, and it's on the leading edge of the bill. The direction of travel is toward the front of the cap, like this." He pointed at me and then reversed his finger so that it was pointing at the bill of the cap as he held it up. "That means that Peter Nicholson wasn't wearing this cap when he was shot; his killer was.... You're... not surprised."

I smiled, looked at Joanne, then at Kate—her eyes were wide. "Surprised?" I said. "A little, but I sure as hell was hoping, too. I spent half the morning and most of the last two weeks trying to figure out what the hell happened that day, and I just couldn't. So I went over the photographs again and again: nothing. Then I noticed the cap lying on the ground *behind* the body. Just how far, I couldn't exactly tell, but I figured at least ten feet. Then it struck me: it was in the wrong place. Think about it. He fell forward onto his face, yeah? If he had, his cap would have come off, but it would have landed in front of him, not behind. So I figured maybe it wasn't his cap at all, and if it wasn't, it probably belonged to the killer."

I looked sideways at Kate. She was shaking her head.

"What?" I asked her.

"Damn it, Harry. I never would have spotted that...."

"You would have if you'd studied the photos as much as I did."

"So, Mike," she said. "The hairs from the cap. We have DNA, right?"

He nodded.

"How long will it take?"

"Two, maybe three weeks."

"Have you sent them off yet?" I asked, mentally crossing my fingers.

"Nope. I was going to do it after you'd gone."

"I'll do it," I said taking the evidence bag from him. "I'll send them to DDC. I can get it done quicker. One week, maybe less."

"But—"

"It's okay, Mike. The chain of custody was broken years ago. Now it's all academic. Helpful, but circumstantial at best. How long before you get the results back for the hairs you found in the truck?"

"Hmmm." He flipped the pages of his desk calendar. "I sent them off on the nineteenth, so... the results should be back... by the eighth?"

"So," I said. "Today's the third. If I get this cap off to DDC this afternoon, I should have the results back by Friday the tenth. Kate, we need DNA samples from Judge Warren, Heath Myers, and Alex Harrison."

"Hah. Good luck with that one. How are you going to pull that off?"

"Well, I was hoping you might help. Look, we know one of those three killed Peter Nicholson, and probably Helen Nicholson too. I'm pretty sure the cap belonged to Ellis Warren. He was wearing a white cap that day...."

"How the hell do you know that?" Kate asked.

"I asked Heath Myers. He remembered. He also told me Nicholson wasn't wearing a cap, that he never wore one, didn't like them; they spoiled his hair."

"He talked to you?" she asked skeptically.

"I thought he might. I never liked him for it, so I figured he had nothing to hide and so might be willing to talk, and he was. But that aside, we have, or will have, DNA from the truck that killed Helen, and from this golf cap, but without DNA from our suspects to compare it to, it's useless. We need samples. So, Kate, can you help?"

She dropped her chin, closed her eyes, and thought; her ponytail flopped over her shoulder, hiding her face. Then she looked up and said, "Jeez, Harry. You're asking a lot. I'll help, but how the hell do we do it?"

I nodded. She was right. It was asking a lot, but it had to be done.

"As I said, I like Warren for it, so Amanda and I will tackle him. I'll find out from August when they're next scheduled to play together and I'll make sure we're there when they come off the course. August will invite us for drinks and I'll get it then. Myers may not be a problem. I don't think it was him. He was quite cooperative earlier. After I have Warren's I'll just flat out ask him for a swab. If he has nothing to hide, and I don't think he does, he'll do it. If he's innocent, he'll want us to know, right?"

She nodded. "So that leaves me with Harrison, then. Christ, Harry. The man's a US attorney. How the hell am I supposed to pull that off?"

I grinned at her. "You'll think of something. He sure as hell is not going to let me near him."

She sighed, a big one. "Okay. I'll think of something. I wonder what we have going on in the department that I can go to him for." She shook her head. "It may take a few days, but I'll get you what you need."

I turned to Willis. "You have more for us, right?"

"I don't, but Joanne does. Joanne?"

"Yes, well." She picked up the gun from the desk, looked first at Kate, then at me. "This weapon did not kill Peter Nicholson."

Okay. I already knew that.

"And I can also tell you that he wasn't killed with a 12-gauge shotgun."

Whoa. That's a new one.

"What? Are you sure about that?" I asked.

"Positive. For several reasons. The most compelling being that I was unable to replicate the wound or the scal-

loping. The shells recovered from Nicholson's gun—one
fired and one live—and from his vest pocket were all
identical 2¾-inch, Winchester 1¼-ounce, number four
12-gauge shells. There are 135 number four pellets to the
ounce, so those particular shells would have held 168."

She placed the gun back on the desk and continued,
"Just to be sure, I bought a box—same brand, same size—
and I opened three of them and counted the number of
shot; each held exactly 168 pieces, but we have only 152
pieces: 147 in the plastic bottle and the 5 Doc Sheddon
recovered from the body. Thus, if he'd been shot with his
own gun, we're short 16 pellets. Even if the gun had been
fired from five feet, the scalloping indicates that *none* of
the shot could have missed the body, and we know from
the X-rays Doc made that there are none left inside the
body. That also indicates he was not killed with his
own gun.

"Now, as I said, I was unable to replicate the wound
using this gun, and I tried; believe me, I tried. Oh, and by
the way, Harry. You owe me two hundred bucks for three
pigskins, and I got a deal on them at Larry's Pork Skins. I
hope that was okay."

"You know it was. So tell us."

"Okay, here we go. We know from the scalloping
around the wound that the shot was made from three to
five feet away—the end of the barrels, that is. That would
put the trigger some five and half feet to seven and a half
feet from the victim. Anyway, I stretched the skins on
some homemade frames that the maintenance department made up for me. I used this gun, fixed to a rig—one

of my own, loaded with identical Winchester shells to those found in the gun—to fire six shots at varying distances ranging between three and five feet. To reproduce a wound, of the same shape and with more or less the same pattern of scalloping, I had to fire the gun at a distance of exactly forty-one inches, roughly three and a half feet. And at a stretch we could go with that, but here's the problem: the wound itself was way too big. Again, this proves that this is not the gun that killed him. It also proves that the gun that did kill him wasn't a 12-gauge."

"Okay, so you say," I said. "But then what was it?"

"Give me a minute and I'll show you."

She left the office and returned a couple of minutes later holding a second shotgun. It looked almost identical to the one on the desk, but I knew that it couldn't be.

"This," she said, holding it up with both hands, "is a Browning Citori 16.... A 16-gauge shotgun, with which I *was* able to replicate the wound pretty closely. My experiments with the pigskin show direction and angle of shot, the shape and size of the wound, and an almost identical pattern of scalloping and, by the way, I do have photographs for you, and I've preserved the skins with each shot identified by number and by weapon. If needed, it can all be placed in evidence, and I am prepared to testify to the veracity of my findings.

"So," she continued, "I did some research. Guess what? A 16-gauge, 2¾-inch, 1⅛-ounce, number four shell holds... exactly 152 number four pellets. Voila!" she said, triumphantly, then looked at us each in turn. "No comments?" she asked, somewhat disappointed.

"I believe you," I said, not quite knowing what to make of her revelation, and not quite sure that it changed anything. We already knew he didn't kill himself, that someone else must have done it. The type of gun used—a 16-gauge shotgun—only reinforced the fact. *I wonder what types of guns the three mouseketeers were using that day. If I read it correctly, even if one of them was carrying a 16-gauge, it wouldn't help a whole lot. All we'd have would be an indicator that that person* might *have been the perp, but that's all. It's still circumstantial. Damn!*

"Well," I said. "That's all very interesting, but...."

"Hell, as far as I can see," Kate said, "it's just one more wrinkle in the cloth that needs smoothing out. We already knew he didn't kill himself. All this does is show us how he might have been killed. But as for who...." She shrugged.

"Okay folks," I said, rising to my feet. "Thanks for everything you've done. I need to do some thinking. In the meantime, Joanne, I'll send you a check for the two hundred. Again, thank you for that."

Kate accompanied me to the elevator and down to the lobby on the first floor. Neither of us spoke on the way down. It wasn't until we reached my car on the far side of the lot that she spoke.

"Harry. It all hinges on the DNA, right?"

"Yup. I'm afraid so. Everything else is just... fluff. 16-gauge or not, I'm still convinced it was one of the three that killed him, and Helen, and I've still got my money on

Ellis Warren. He not only had the most to gain by killing Peter—Mary Ann—but also the most to lose if he didn't—possible exposure for insider trading, though that's also conjecture at this point; I've got Ronnie digging into it.... We need those samples, Kate."

She nodded. "I'll do my best. Talk to you next week, Harry. Give Amanda my best, okay?" And she turned and walked back into the police department.

Me? I returned to my office, had Jacque priority overnight the golf cap to Lindsey Oats at DDC, and then left. It was just after noon and I'd had enough. The only place I wanted to be was Lookout Mountain, with a little homemade cottage pie, a couple of shots of Laphroaig, and Amanda.

27

MONDAY, FEBRUARY 6, 9:00 A.M

My plan for the weekend was to clear my head, put the case out of my mind for a couple of days, but I couldn't. I spent most of the weekend going over my notes, the evidence—photographs, reports, etc., and by the time Monday morning rolled around I was more convinced than ever that Ellis Warren had indeed murdered Peter Nicholson.

Did he murder Helen Nicholson too? I had a hard time believing *that*, but what other answer could there be? What motive could there be? Fear of what Peter's second autopsy might reveal? That was a nonstarter; the autopsy had revealed nothing we didn't already know, or suspect. But then again, criminals think differently from regular folks. Most of them make mistakes of one sort or another. In the past, I've found that guilt can drive the imagination wild, and a killer to try to cover up evidence that may not even exist. But a circuit court judge?

It wouldn't be the first time, and they put their clothes

on the same way everybody else does. And Ellis Warren
sure as hell has a lot to lose.

There was no doubt that Warren didn't want to give
up Mary Ann, and we knew that Nicholson had given
Mary Ann an ultimatum—and that she'd agreed to give
up her affair with Warren. Then there was the insider
trading thing. Were they guilty of that? If so, we'd probably never know, but if Nicholson threatened to expose
him... if he didn't want to lose her.... Double motive. But
was he desperate enough to kill Nicholson over it? Did he
shoot him in the heart with his 16-gauge shotgun or was
there another solution? Did he even *own* a 16-gauge
shotgun?

There's no mention in the reports of who was shooting
what in the reports, either. Sloppy, sloppy, sloppy. Israel
Friggin' Hands! Someone should have checked those guns.

But if Warren did have a 16-gauge, I'll bet he still
does. Guns are like children. We hate to give 'em up.

I flipped through the pages of the notes taken that
day in 2002, and the reports, and I watched the videos
for... I dunno, what must have been the tenth time, and I
learned no more than I already knew, which wasn't a
whole hell of a lot.

And nowhere could I find any references to shotguns
other than the one found under Nicholson's body.

I looked at my watch. It was just after ten o'clock. I
sat there for several minutes debating whether or not I
should drive to Atlanta and try to talk to Israel Hands. In
the end, though, I decided it would be a waste of time.

The man had hated my guts *before* I put him away, and it was hardly likely he'd talk to me now, or even see me.

Ron Fowler, though. Now there's a thought. I need to get out of here anyway, get some fresh air. That gas heat is killing me.

TEN MINUTES later I was parked outside Ron Fowler's tri-level on Cloverdale Loop. I saw the curtain move and decided I'd better do the same.

I locked the car and walked the path to the front door. Before I could thumb the bell, however, the door opened and there he was. I might have stepped back in time three weeks, for he was wearing the exact same jeans and plaid flannel shirt as he had been before, or else ones just like them.

"Come on in, Harry. I was hoping you might drop by again. I saw that they'd dug him up, Nicholson, and I was curious to know what you found. Sit down, man. Sit down. You want some coffee? I just made some."

"Sure. Why not. A little cream, no sugar."

"So what's going on?" he asked, sitting down at the kitchen table across from me. "I never thought I'd see the day. What did they find?"

"Not much, Ron, unfortunately. Tell me," I continued, "how well do you remember that day in the forest?"

He shrugged, squinted at me across the table. "Like it was yesterday. I still can't believe how they handled it.

Maybe Doc Bowden just couldn't be bothered. It weren't no accident, Harry."

"Yeah, Ron. I know. It was sloppily handled at best, and a criminal cover up at worst."

"Hey, Harry. Go easy, will ya? Israel called the shots. We did as we were told. He and the doc said it was an accident, so an accident it was. You didn't screw with Israel, you know that; you know what a rat's ass he could be."

I nodded. He was right. Hands had been a law unto himself.

"Ron, could one of those three have been paying him off?"

He looked down his nose at me, squinted, shook his head, slowly. "I... don't know. Could have been. There was some talk. He was a crooked son of a bitch. There was one time—"

"Look, that's actually not why I'm here. You say you remember that day well, right?"

He nodded.

"Okay, so which one of them had a 16-gauge?"

"A what?"

"A 16-gauge shotgun?"

"Whoa. That's not one I expected. Lemme think a minute." And he did. He closed his eyes and he thought, for a long time. So long I thought he'd fallen asleep.

"None of them," he said eventually.

"...What?"

"You heard me. None of them had a 16-gauge. They all had 12-gauges, fancy 12-gauges. That's how I know. I figured that between the four of them, they were carrying close to a hundred thousand bucks worth of shotguns."

"You must have it wrong, Ron. One of those three was carrying a 16-gauge. Peter Nicholson was killed with a...." *Damn. I've said too much.*

His eyes were wide. "No way! I don't believe it."

"Ron. I never said that, you hear? You can't let it out. If you do, you'll screw up the investigation."

"Harry? Look at me. Look me in the eye."

I did.

"I was a cop, remember? A good cop. I know how it works. I won't say a word; you have my word on it. But a 16-gauge you say? You've got to be shittin' me. Nope. I swear it, Harry. They were all carrying 12-gauges."

I leaned back in my chair. *Christ. If what he says is true, it makes Doc and Snyder look like a couple of clowns. Say it ain't so, Ron. Say it ain't so.*

"Ron," I said, shaking my head. "Joanne Snyder is prepared to testify that Nicholson was shot with a 16-guage loaded with number four shot."

"Then she'd be wrong. They was all of them carrying 12-gauges. I'd swear to it."

"Well," I said, more than a little pissed off, "that means one of two things: either Joanne is wrong, or it wasn't one of them that killed her."

"Sorry, Harry."

"Sheesh. That's all I needed. Now what?"

He simply shook his head.

I told him goodbye and left, wishing to hell that I hadn't seen him. *Damn! Damn! Damn!*

I sat for a minute inside the Maxima outside his home, thinking, then I dialed Joanne Snyder's direct number at the PD.

"Joanne. This is Harry Starke. I have a problem."

"Tell me about it."

"Look, I've just spent the last thirty minutes with Ron Fowler. He was one of the detectives on the Nicholson case back in '02. He swears they were all carrying 12-gauge guns, that there wasn't a 16-gauge between them. Are you sure you got it right?"

That was met with stony silence.

I sighed. "Sorry, Joanne, but I had to ask."

"Yes, well. Call me if you need me." And with that, she hung up, and I felt.... Well, not good, that's for sure, and I drove away from Cloverdale Loop wondering what the hell I was going to do next.

Next, I called Kate. "Hey," I said when she picked up. "I had questions, so I went to see Ron Fowler again. He was one of the detectives on the case back in 2002. I told you. Remember?"

"I remember. I also remember you told me the whole thing was shoved under the rug. Was he responsible for that?"

"No, just the opposite, in fact. He never did believe Nicholson's death was an accident, but Israel Hands closed the investigation before it had even started. Anyway, look. I have a problem. I wanted to run it by you. Okay?"

"Sure. Go ahead."

"Joanne Snyder's inspection of the wound, and her

experiments, indicate he was killed with a 16-gauge shot-gun, not a 12-gauge. That's why I went to see Fowler. I found no record of the other three guns ever being taken into evidence, or any reference in any of the reports as to who was carrying what. One of the three had to have been using a 16-gauge, right?"

"Makes sense."

"Right, but who? It was a long shot, but I figured Fowler might remember, and he did, and therein lies the problem. He swears that none of them were using 16-gauges, that they all were carrying 12-gauges."

"Yep. You do have a problem. So what's the answer?"

"One of two: either Fowler made a mistake or...."

"Or Joanne did," she finished for me. "Oh please tell me you didn't."

"I did, and she's pissed, but I had to ask her. There were only three people with Nicholson in Prentice Cooper that day and one of them killed him. So one of them, Joanne or Fowler, made a mistake."

She was silent for a moment, then, "You think?"

"Come on, Kate. Had to be."

"My money's on Fowler. Look, Harry. You know as much about shotguns as I do, which isn't a whole lot, and I'd bet Fowler's the same. There's very little difference, as far as I know, between a 16-gauge and a 12-gauge. They look practically identical. He made a mistake. One of them had to be a 16-gauge. Had to."

"Yeah, I guess you're right. I don't see Joanne screwing it up, so there's no other answer, unless there were more than four of them there that day, and there's no record of anyone else. If there had been... well, there couldn't have; we'd know."

"I talked to Mike a few minutes ago," she said after a moment. "He said we should have the DNA back on the hairs from the truck either Thursday or Friday. I asked him to call the lab and give 'em a push. He said he would. Any news from your DNA lab?"

"No. I had Jacque FedEx the sample to them before we left on Friday. I'm paying for a rush job, so I should have something back by the weekend. In the meantime, we need those samples. Have you figured out how you're going to get Harrison's?"

"Nope, but I will. As soon as I get it, I'll let you know. Gotta go, Harry. It's busier in here than a Chinese sweatshop. Later, okay?"

I told her yeah, and she disconnected. I wanted to go home, but I had too much on my mind.

So, without a 16-gauge, what the hell do I have? A couple of hairs in a damned hat, if that. The way things are going, they probably belong to Peter Nicholson's cat.

In the meantime, I need to figure out how to get samples from Warren and Myers. Warren shouldn't be too difficult. He's playing nine holes with August on Wednesday; they're having lunch together. I'll maybe be able to pick up something from the table. Myers, though....

I hesitated for a moment, and then looked up Heath Myers's phone number.

"Heath. It's Harry Starke. You got a minute?"

"Damn it. Not again. What do you want this time?"

"Look, Heath. I think I'm close to closing this Peter

Nicholson thing out. You told me you had nothing to do with his death, and I believe you. Thing is, though, it all comes down to DNA...."

I waited for a response. I got none.

"You still there, Heath?"

"Yeah, I'm still here. And the answer's no."

"Jeez, you don't even know what I was going to ask."

"Yeah, I do. You want me to give you a DNA sample. The answer is... *no!*"

"Now why the hell not? If you had nothing to do with it, why wouldn't you?"

"Look, I had that slimy little bulldog from Channel 7 here only this morning, asking questions—loaded questions. I gave him nothing, but when did that ever stop 'em making shit up, destroying people's reputations? You got a big mouth, Starke, and you like the attention, so no. Now leave me the hell alone." And he hung up.

Well, so much for that. How the hell am I going to get it?

28

WEDNESDAY, FEBRUARY 8, 11:45 A.M

Two days later, I still hadn't figured out how I was going to get a DNA sample from Heath Myers. I'd considered going through his trash, but I hadn't sunk quite that low... yet. As for Ellis Warren, I decided to take Amanda to lunch at the club that Wednesday. She was back at Channel 7, but for a possible story she was able to get an extended lunch break.

We arrived at the club around 11:45 and found August, Warren, and... Mary Ann.

Damn it. August should know better.

Barely had we walked into the lounge when my father spotted us. I'd already made him aware of what I wanted, and he'd agreed to play along.

"Harry!" He stood and waved us over; I glanced at Mary Ann. *Uh oh, this could get ugly.*

"Harry, Amanda, join us," he said as we arrived table-side. Hah. You should have seen the look Mary Ann gave him. I smiled, inwardly of course, and almost declined, but then I thought how much fun it would be to spend a little time playing with them. So we did; we joined them.

I thought Mary Ann was going to have a conniption fit; her husband wasn't too happy either. Just to stoke the fire a little more, I took the seat next to her. She recoiled like a snake confronted by a mongoose.

"So," I said brightly, "how did it go, Ellis? Dad beat you again?" I could tell by the look on his face that I'd hit a nerve... or maybe it was something else. Whatever. He didn't answer, but August did.

"Not by much, just a couple of holes, and he hasn't paid up yet, have you Ellis? You owe me a hundred." Not so subtle, that, but August never was one to beat around the bush.

So Ellis pulled out his wallet and flipped a single bill across the table. August grabbed it and, with no little relish, waved it in the air to attract George.

"Drinks on me," he said loudly, then, "No! The drinks are on Ellis. Bombay gin and tonic for me, and whatever these good folks would like." He handed the bill to George, telling him to let him know when it was gone.

"Such bad manners," Mary Ann whispered under her breath, but making sure it was loud enough for me to hear. I simply grinned at her; the sneer I received in return would have curdled fresh cream. She could be volatile, Mary Ann, and I wasn't at the top of her popularity list.

Now lunch at the club, on any day, is a fairly casual affair, and that Wednesday was no different to any other

—slightly slower, if anything, and lunch at our table went even slower, the atmosphere was... frosty would be putting it mildly. Finally, though, it was over. August had the bill put on his account and the Warrens said their thanks and got up to leave; August went with them, leaving us alone at the table.

I had my back to the door and I didn't want to turn around, so I watched Amanda as she watched them go. She nodded and, using two fingers on the inside, I picked up Warren's glass. Shielding what I was doing from the room, I took a paper evidence bag from my pocket and dropped the glass inside, and we were out of there.

One down, two to go. Now I needed a sample from Myers.

29

THURSDAY, FEBRUARY 9, 8:00 A.M

I was on edge that following morning. I hadn't slept a whole lot; in fact, I'd watched the clock for most of the night. At one point I stepped out onto the patio to try to relieve the tension. It was a beautiful night, but cold as hell, and all I managed to do was wake myself up even more. Finally, around four in the morning, I gave up, dressed in sweats, and headed out on East Brow Road. I don't remember much about that run; I was lost in thought, trying to put a face to my killer, but all I got was shadows—ghostly, featureless images that taunted and teased but did little other than deepen my feelings of inadequacy. How far I ran that morning, I have no idea, but I was gone for more than an hour, and when I returned I was sweating like a pig, and Amanda was waiting for me, a look of deep concern on her face.

I took to the shower, spent fifteen minutes under the hot deluge, and emerged feeling somewhat better.

We had breakfast together and then I left for the

office early, way too early. When I arrived I realized I'd left my office keys at home. Hah! A great start to the day. I sat in the car for almost thirty minutes before Jacque arrived and let me in, and by the time she did, just before eight, I was in a filthy mood. Yes, I could have called her, but... hell, it wasn't her fault. She was followed, one by one, by the rest of the crew, and by eight everyone was at work... except me. I, as usual those days, had nothing to do. And so, from eight until ten o'clock, I harassed my poor employees mercilessly, and then the FedEx van arrived.

I grabbed the package from the driver and, grinning, but full of trepidation, I went to my office and slammed the door behind me, yelling at Jacque to hold my calls and that I wasn't to be disturbed.

I slit open the package and pulled out a sheaf of reports from DDC. I set them in a pile in front of me and then settled down to study them. What I read was really no surprise.

First, the DNA reports on the hairs and blood in and on the cap found near Peter Nicholson's body. Lindsey had compared the hairs to the sample taken from his body at the second autopsy, and the blood spatter on the side of Peter's shotgun. The blood samples from the cap and the Browning were a match, indicating that they all had been generated by the single shot that killed Peter. She had also compared his sample DNA with the hairs found in the cap: no match—the hairs did not belong to Peter, as I had expected.

But that's good. Now we know. Now all I need to do is figure out who they belong to.

I had a copy of Lindsey's report on the hair found in the cap copied, and then I had Leslie deliver it to Mike Willis, and then I waited impatiently for him to call me, which he eventually did. It was almost noon.

The DNA results from the hairs found in the truck had arrived in his office at around the same time FedEx had delivered mine. He confirmed the match: both samples—the hairs from the truck and from the cap—came from the same person. So now we knew for certain we were looking for one killer. Unfortunately, we still needed samples to compare them with.

I had Warren's sample, and I knew that by then it was already in Lindsey's lab at DDC. I still hadn't managed to obtain a sample from Myers, but I wasn't too worried about it. If I needed one—and I was pretty sure I wouldn't—I'd figure out a way to get it later. No, I was all but certain Heath Myers had had nothing to do with Peter Nicholson's 'accident,' or the horrific death of Peter's mother. Don't ask me why; it was just a gut feeling I couldn't get rid of. No, my money was on Ellis Warren. The only other possible suspect was Alex Harrison. Now all I needed was for Kate to pull through with a sample from him.

As if in answer to a psychic message, there was a knock on my office door. It opened, and Kate walked in.

With no ceremony whatsoever, she deposited a small plastic evidence bag on the desk in front of me. Inside, I could see a piece of well-chewed gum.

I looked up at her. "Harrison?"

She nodded.

"Wow. How did you manage that? Wait. Jacque!" I called. "First I need to get this on its way to DDC." So I sent it off with Jacque, then called Lindsey and told her it was on its way and to put a rush on the report. That done, I turned to Kate, who was now seated across from me.

"So," I said. "How *did* you get it? How the hell did you get in to see him?"

"You know, Harry... I couldn't come up with a single believable reason why I needed to make an appointment to the United States attorney, not without making him suspicious, so I just went over there and knocked on his door. Told him I was passing and wanted to say hello. It was just that easy. Alex has always had a thing for me. Anyway, he offered me coffee and I accepted. Now, unfortunately, I'm committed to having lunch with him tomorrow. He really is a tedious man."

I smiled and shook my head. I could just imagine his reaction when she walked in the door.

"And the chewing gum?" I asked.

"A gift from the gods. I asked to use his restroom; he's big wheel, has one of his own. I was hoping I might get a hair sample, but there wasn't a comb... but then I noticed the wastebasket next to the sink. What can I say? It's not admissible, but if the result of the DNA test is positive, we should be able to get a warrant for... well, for *some-thing*.... Or I can just steal his napkin after coffee tomorrow. That would be admissible."

"We still don't have a sample from Myers, but we did

get one from Warren, though he doesn't know it, and that one is admissible. Great minds think alike: I grabbed his glass from the table after he'd left. I've already sent it to the lab. We should have results back from both samples in a few days."

Sheesh. It's a good thing Helen paid up front. We must be into DDC for eight or nine grand by now.

She nodded, then frowned and said, "What about the gun, Harry?"

And right then and there, a deep gloom descended on my shoulders. I knew exactly what she was asking.

"The one that killed Peter Nicholson?"

"Yeah. Joanne came to me earlier this morning. She's not happy. She's a little upset that you're doubting her findings."

I shook my head. "I really need to apologize to her. It's not that I doubt her; it's just that what she found doesn't fit neatly into my package. I mean, a 16-gauge? I dunno, Kate."

"Harry. If Joanne says he was killed with one, he was. You can take it to the bank."

I nodded. "So Fowler had to be mistaken. Hell, Kate. The man was adamant, but if he was wrong...."

"If he was wrong, who the hell was carrying a 16-gauge that day?" She finished for me.

"It had to have been Warren," I said. "I don't like Myers for it... or even Harrison, but... ah! How the hell do we find out?"

"We need to go looking for a 16-gauge shotgun—at the Warrens', first. Then...." She trailed off, unsure.

"Sure, but we have no probable cause. We have no DNA matches for anything, at least not yet. Still, I hate sitting around on my hands, waiting. I wonder...."

"What?"

"I need to make a call."

And so I did.

"Henry?" I said when he picked up.

Judge Strange? Kate mouthed. I nodded and smiled.

"Hey, Harry. How the hell are you?"

"I'm good, Henry...."

He waited.

"Henry, you remember telling me that if I thought there was anything you could do to help with the Nicholson case, you would?"

"Ye-es...."

"Well, I do, and there is... something. I need your help. I need a warrant to search Ellis Warren's house."

I winced. I could imagine the stunned look he must have had on his face, and his silence only confirmed it.

Finally: "Go on, Harry."

"I have the DNA results back on the cap they found near the body—the hairs in the cap—and the hairs they found inside the truck that killed Helen Nicholson; they *do* match. Whoever killed Nicholson also killed Helen."

"So..." he said cautiously, "what you're telling me is that you don't have anyone to match them to?"

"No. Not yet—"

"Then...."

"Yeah, I know, but I have Myers on record and he swears that Warren was the only one wearing a white cap

that day, and that Nicholson wasn't wearing one at all."
Oh hell. I hope I can get away with this.

"You have him on record? How on record?"

Oh he's sharp, is Henry.

I sighed, then said, quietly, "I recorded the conversation."

I looked at Kate; she was gobsmacked.

Henry was silent for a moment. "And he doesn't know you recorded the conversation, I assume."

"No. He doesn't. And, Henry, you know better than I that Tennessee is a one-party consent state. I didn't have to tell him. Jeez, Henry. You know Myers. He wouldn't have talked to me if I had."

"Relax, Harry. You doth protest too much, methinks. It was unethical of you, yes, but legal? Also yes. So why do you want the warrant?"

"Okay, so Warren was wearing a white cap. A white cap was found at the scene with Peter Nicholson's blood on it, and hairs inside it are a DNA match to hairs found in the truck that killed Helen, which means that whoever was wearing that cap that day killed both of them.... And I'm looking for..." I hesitated "...the shotgun. A 16-gauge shotgun. Okay," I said quickly, "before you say no, the gun goes with the cap, and the hairs; we know that Peter Nicholson was killed by a shot from a 16-gauge. I need to find that gun, and I think it belongs to Warren. If he was wearing the cap that we know the killer was wearing.... He has to own the gun too."

"Oh, Harry. Harry, Harry. That's mighty thin, mighty thin indeed...."

I waited silently while he thought about it.

"Harry, if I didn't know you.... If I wasn't sure you had all your ducks in a row and quacking fit to be tied, I wouldn't even entertain it. As it is.... Have Kate write it up the way you want it, and I'll sign it. And I want a copy of that recording. Don't know if it's enough to cover my ass if Ellis decides to object, but it will have to do."

"Thanks, Henry. We'll drop by later."

"Yes, you do that." He hung up, and I looked at Kate. I was smiling; she wasn't.

"You sneaky son of a.... I hope to hell we find it. If we don't, we'll have one, no *two* irate judges to deal with. I'll go write up the warrant. You coming with me or what?"

"What do you think?"

I was already getting up from my desk.

THURSDAY, FEBRUARY 9, 2:00 P.M

It was just after two o'clock that afternoon when Kate knocked on Ellis Warren's front door. We had arrived in force: Kate's official car and two cruisers, each containing two uniformed officers.

"Hello Judge Warren," she said when he opened the door. "I have a warrant to search the house, garage, and any outbuildings. We're looking for a 16-gauge shotgun. Do you own such a weapon?"

"What the hell?" He snatched the papers from her hand. "Who the hell issued this?" He scanned the document. "Hah! I might have known, Judge Henry Strange." He looked over Kate's shoulder at me. "Starke. You have a hand in this, you son of a bitch. Okay. You got your warrant, but you're not a sworn officer; you're not setting a foot inside my house. Lieutenant— whatever your name is, you and your officers may enter, but not him."

He glared at me; I smiled back at him. "That's fine

with me. I can wait out here, where the neighbors can watch...."

"Damn it! Damn you! Come in, all of you. Starke, you stay in the foyer, and not a foot further."

The foyer, if it could be called that, was about an acre of open space—yes, I'm exaggerating—that provided access to the living room beyond, a formal dining room immediately to the right, a huge kitchen to the right of the living room, and a winding staircase to the left. Beyond that, I assumed, were several more ground floor rooms. And it was in the foyer that Kate assembled her team. While this was going on the judge stood impatiently by and watched; Mary Ann was nowhere to be seen.

"Is Mrs. Warren at home?" Kate asked. "If so, I'd like you to ask her to join us."

"She's not here. She's out of town for a few days visiting her mother."

She nodded. "So, Judge Warren. I'll ask you again: Do you have one or more 16-gauge shotguns here in the house or anywhere else?"

"We do. There's one in my study, in the gun safe, along with my other guns. I never use it though, never have. I don't like it. It's neither a 12-gauge nor a 20-gauge, something odd, in between. I don't think it's ever been shot. I'll get it for you."

"If you don't mind, sir. I'll come with you. I'd rather you didn't touch it... again."

"Again? Again, you say? I haven't touched the damned thing in twenty years or more. The only reason I keep it is because it belonged to my father. It's worth...

well, I don't know, quite a lot, I should imagine. He gave it to me just before he died, back in December of '98. I locked it away and haven't touched it since."

I watched as Kate pulled on a pair of latex gloves, and then they went off together. Two minutes later, they returned; Kate held the gun, a custom Browning Sweet Sixteen, with both hands. It was indeed a beautiful weapon. The barrel and furniture gleamed in the soft lights, the gold inlay on the chamber bright and sharp.

Too bright? Recently cleaned? I wonder.

"This is the only 16-gauge shotgun you own, Judge Warren?" Kate asked.

"It is. Look, I know why you're doing this. I was given a copy of the autopsy and ballistics reports by John Dooley. It claims that Peter was killed with a 16-gauge shotgun. That's preposterous. We all carried 12-gauges that day. I don't think Heath and Alex even own 16-gauges. Your ballistics person must have made a mistake. He fell on his gun. I was there, damn it. Hell, I wasn't but a few yards away when I heard Heath yelling. He must have been dead for... I don't know... several minutes at least. We were still in the woods when we heard the shots.... Oh my, I never realized. I thought it must have been.... I was on my way to the trailhead...."

"So," I said, "just to be clear. The last shot you heard was, what, five minutes, two minutes before Myers found him? Is that what you're saying?"

For a minute, I thought he wasn't going to answer, but then he nodded and said, thoughtfully, "Five. Five minutes at most. No more than that."

I looked at the shotgun in Kate's hands. "That needs to go to Mike Willis," I said. "I doubt he'll find anything, but it's worth a try."

"Oh, I don't know," she said. "Take a look." And she held it out so that I could see the ends of the barrels. They were clean, really clean—and then I saw it. About a half inch down inside the bottom barrel was a tiny spec of... something, and I looked at her and nodded.

"What? What is it?" Warren asked.

"Probably nothing," Kate said. "We'll see. You're sure this is the only 16-gauge you own?"

"How many times do I have to tell you? *Yes*, damn it. It's the only one."

"Fine," she replied. "I'll give you a receipt for it and we'll be on our way." She did, and thanked him, and we left him standing on the top step of his front porch, staring after us.

"We need to get the gun to Mike Willis and have him harvest whatever that is in there," I said. "When you've got it, call Jacque and have her give you our FedEx number and then send the sample overnight to DDC." I looked at my watch. It was almost a quarter after three. "If he can get it done quickly, there's still time to get it to FedEx for delivery by ten tomorrow morning. I'll call Lindsey and ask her to rush it."

"Shouldn't we send it to our lab?"

"Sure, if you want to wait for a month. Look, this weapon is part of my investigation. It has nothing to do with Helen's death, although it might when we get the results back, so let's get it done quick and easy, without all the bureaucracy, okay?"

"Okay then. It's your money."

"No, it's Helen's. And it's what she would have wanted."

Kate dropped me back at the office and then went about getting the shotgun to Mike Willis. I waited as long as I could stand it, then picked up the phone and called him.

"Hey, Mike. What was that crap on the inside of the 16-gauge? Did you figure it out?"

"What? What crap...? Oh, that crap. Yes. I told Kate I'd give you a call. It's already on its way to DDC."

"You were going to call me? Hell, Mike, it's been two hours. When were you going to call, for Christ's sake?"

"Um, yeah. Sorry. I've been busy."

"*So?*"

"It's human tissue, Harry. Old, but it's still viable, I'm sure."

Jeez! Thank you, Lord. "Okay, Mike. And... sorry I jumped on you. I'm antsy as hell right now. I owe you one —no I owe you a lot, and my heartfelt thanks for all you do. You're a good friend. Thanks."

"Oh, hey. You don't need to apologize; we're good. You know that. Anytime, Harry. Anytime."

31

FRIDAY, FEBRUARY 17, 9:00 A.M

The next week dragged on and on. The weather was terrible again. There still wasn't much to do at the office.... Ah, there was a high-end divorce case I could have taken, but I'd quit chasing erring husbands a long time ago and I wasn't about to start up again.

I took a lot of time off that week. I played some golf—not as much as I would have liked, just eighteen holes on Tuesday, the one sunny day we'd had in I couldn't remember how long—but the ground was soggy, the greens slow, and the bunkers might as well have been beaches at low tide: the sand was wet and cloying. I went to the range and practiced until my fingers hurt: yes, I shoot with both hands. I took Amanda to lunch most days, and when she couldn't make it, I took either Kate or Jacque. By the time Friday rolled around, I was wound tighter than an eight-day clock.

But Friday did arrive, finally, as it always does, and it

quickly turned into the blackest day of the new year, at least for me: the rest of the DNA results from Lindsey at DDC arrived.

It was just after nine o'clock that morning when Jacque dumped the bulky FedEx package on my desk. It contained the DNA reports on the human tissue taken from the inside of the barrel of the 16-gauge Browning, and on the samples we'd taken from Harrison and Warren.

I was grinning to myself, the proverbial cat who ate the cream, as I slit open the package and extracted the contents and began to read through the reports. Then, slowly, the more I read... the grin turned into a frown, and then a scowl. I couldn't believe what I was reading: the comparison reports were devastating. Other than the tissue sample from the gun, which matched the sample taken at Peter's second autopsy, there were no matches: no match between Warren and the hairs in the cap. No match between Harrison and the hairs in the cap. And no match between either of them and the hairs in the truck. *What the hell?*

I couldn't bring myself to believe it. It had to be Warren. Nicholson's tissue, his DNA, inside the barrel of Warren's Browning 16-gauge *proved* that it had to be him. It was his friggin' gun, for Christ's sake.

Something was way out of whack. The white cap, the Sweet Sixteen, both Warren's. The hairs.... *Christ!*

Well, I couldn't place him inside the truck that killed Helen, but I sure as hell could place him and his gun at the scene of Peter Nicholson's murder. But the cap? The hairs? And if not Warren or Harrison, who the hell could they could belo—*Oh hell no. Not in a million years. Could they? Yeah! They could, damn it. Why didn't I think of that before?*

I called Kate, and then I called Judge Strange. I told them both what I was thinking and what I thought we needed to do to put this thing to bed. Next I called Sheriff Steve Walker and told him what I was planning, and I asked him to join me; the Peter Nicholson killing was, after all, a county case. To say he was surprised to get the call would be the king of all understatements. He questioned me at length, but in the end, a little reluctantly, he agreed to join us.

32

FRIDAY FEBRUARY 17, 3:30 P.M

K ate picked me up at three thirty that afternoon. She was driving her unmarked Crown Vic and had two uniformed officers in the back seat, leaving the front seat for me, and we drove to Riverview and the Warren house.

"So," I said. "Do you have the warrants?"

She smiled at me. "I do. Do you think we have our killer?"

I smiled back at her. "I do."

Steve Walker was waiting for us when we arrived outside the Warren home.

"Good afternoon, Judge," Kate said when he opened the door. "We'd like to talk to you about the murders of Peter and Helen Nicholson. I'm not formally pressing charges, but you might like to have your attorney present. Would you like to call him? We can wait while you do."

"My attorney? What the hell are you talking about?" he asked as he backed into the foyer. We followed him in.

"What the hell's going on here? And what are you doing here, Sheriff?"

"I think maybe you *do* need a lawyer, Judge," Sheriff Walker said. "I really do!"

"What's going on?" Mary Ann Warren asked.

By now we were inside the vast living room, where she was seated at a small table with her iPhone. She stood as we came in, but Warren waved her down again.

"Don't worry, my dear. Just more damned stuff about Peter. They're not going to be here long, I promise you."

I shook my head. "We know that the gun we took from here last week killed Peter Nicholson, Ellis," I told him quietly.

He looked at me like a bird of paradise had just crapped on his head. I think he was too stunned to answer, so I continued. "You were there that day, so would you like to tell us what the hell happened? The 16-gauge had Nicholson's DNA inside the barrel—blowback—from the shot that killed him, and you know what that means. We also have testimony that you were wearing a white golf cap that day, and we found a white golf cap not ten feet from Nicholson's body. We have sworn testimony from four different witnesses that you were having an affair with Mary Ann at the time of his death, and had been for more than a year before." I turned to look at Mary Ann Warren. "We also know that Peter had persuaded you to stop seeing Ellis. Isn't that true?"

She said nothing. Didn't move. Not even a twitch.

I nodded. "But there was more, wasn't there, Judge.

Nicholson was threatening to expose you to the Securities and Exchange Commission for insider trading if you didn't give her up. That's also true, isn't it?"

"I. Didn't. Kill. Him," he said through clenched teeth.

"You had plenty of reason to, though, didn't you." I stared at him for a long moment, then said, "But I believe you, Ellis. I don't believe you did kill Peter Nicholson." Then I turned to her and said, "Because it was you, wasn't it, Mary Ann."

Her face went white, her mouth dropped open, and for a moment I thought she was going to pass out, or worse, throw up. She didn't do either. Instead she looked down at her hands, and clasped them tightly together in her lap.

"Kate?"

Kate nodded. "Mary Ann Warren, I have a warrant for a sample of your DNA in order to make comparison tests with the DNA taken from hairs found in the white golf cap on May 3, 2002, and hairs found in the truck that was used to kill Helen Nicholson on January 18 of this year. I am now making a formal request that you supply such a sample," she said, taking a small plastic box from her jacket pocket. "Please open your mouth."

"The hell she will," Warren said. "Mary Ann, you keep your mouth shut. I'm calling my attorney. You say nothing and you do *not* give them your DNA...."

"Stop it, Ellis," she said. She was already crying; the tears were rolling freely down her cheeks. "It's over. I knew when I lost my cap that day that they'd figure it out eventually. I couldn't go back for it. I heard you coming. I saw Heath through the trees. You were all too close....

"I... I did love him, you know." She looked up at us through her tears. "It's just that I loved Ellis more. I couldn't give him up, not ever, and I knew Peter would ruin him if I didn't, so... I decided.... Well, you know." She looked down at her hands; her knuckles were white.

"So you killed him?" Kate asked. "You just decided to kill him? How could you do that?"

She looked up again, unclasped her hands, shrugged and, her eyes bright and clear and free of tears, seemingly without remorse, said, "I had no choice."

"And Helen Nicholson?" Kate asked.

She shook her head. "I didn't have a choice there, either. She was going to dig him up and spoil everything. I had to stop her, and I did...." She had a slight smile on her lips and a faraway look in her eyes. "You should have heard the bones crunch."

"Mary Ann Warren...." Kate said, taking her handcuffs from the back pocket of her jeans.

And, well, you know the rest.

FRIDAY, FEBRUARY 17, 9:00 P.M

Later I sat alone in my study, gazing out of the window. The night was cold and clear and the visibility almost infinite. I sipped my scotch, lost in thought—not quite depressed, but filled with a deep sense of loss. The lights of the city below were bright and beautiful; the river was a shimmering silver sash that snaked away into the distance, wrapping itself around the city and then meandering east toward the great towers of the Sequoya nuclear plant just visible as two brightly lit spots on the horizon.

As I reviewed the events of the past few weeks, I couldn't help but think of Helen Nicholson, and I wished I could have given her the news. No, it wasn't good news, but it would have provided closure.

Hell, no it wouldn't. It never does. That's just a load of bull, psychobabble. How the hell does anyone ever get over one of their kids being murdered? How many times have I looked a grieving parent in the eye and wished to hell I was somewhere else, my own parents included? Then my thoughts turned to my kid brother, Henry. He'd been murdered less than a year ago. I knew who did it, and I'd sent him to hell, but did it bring closure? Hell no, and it never would. Henry was gone forever, leaving me and my father and his mother, Rose, with just a few fleeting memories that dimmed with each passing month.

The door opened behind me. I looked around, knowing it was Amanda, and I smiled up at her, patted the space on the sofa beside me. She sat down and I put my arm around her shoulder and pulled her to me.

"You're in one of your moods again, aren't you?" she asked.

I nodded.

"Another case done with and you're suffering from post-partum depression, but it will pass. It always does."

I nodded again, but then thought for a moment and said, "I don't know that it will, this time."

She leaned forward, turned and looked at me, concerned. "Why not? What's wrong, Harry."

I shrugged. "I'm not sure. I feel empty. I don't know what it is. I was thinking of Helen... and Henry... and Dad... and me... and... and you."

"Me? Why me?"

The truth was, even I didn't know. I did know that the death of Helen Nicholson had affected me more than any I could remember, other than Henry's.

"I'm not sure, but I'm thinking I can't go on like this. I've made a lot of enemies over the years. Some are dead.

Some will never see the outside of a prison cell. Some are still out there.... I'm tired, Amanda. I'm tired of constantly looking over my shoulder, wondering. And I worry about you, all the time. And then I think about what happened to Helen and I go cold; my hair prickles on the back of my neck, and I think, 'What if....'" I shrugged again, and pulled her to me.

She put her hand on my chest and pushed, leaned back, and stared into my eyes. "Harry, you can't live like that. *We* can't live like that."

"I know," I said. "I want out, Amanda. I can't do it anymore. I dream about it, about you, and not just at night, but even when I'm awake, alone, like just now. I wake up sweating. It's.... I've seen too much death. Do you have any idea how many homicides I've handled or been involved in over the past seventeen years? No? *I* don't even know; I never did bother to count them, but it's in the hundreds. Hundreds of people dead, and for what?"

"Harry...."

"Yeah, I know. It's what I do, what I chose to do...."

"And now?"

"I don't know. I can't do anything else, and I can't just sit around and wait for God.... I was thinking... about those weeks we spent together in the Islands...."

"Oh come on, Harry. It was wonderful, but neither of us could live like that for very long. We'd go crazy; me more than you. You have to snap out of this."

She took the empty glass from my hand and set it on the table.

"Look at me," she said quietly.

I did.

"It will be all right."

And it was.

At least for a while.

UNTITLED

Thank you.

Thank you for taking the time to read Without Remorse. I hope you enjoyed it,. If you did, please consider posting a short review on Amazon (just a sentence will do). Word of mouth is an author's best friend and much appreciated.

Reviews are so very important. I don't have the backing of a major New York publisher. I can't afford take out ads in the newspapers and on TV, but you can help get the word out.

To those many of my readers who have already posted reviews to this and my other novels, thank you for your past and continued support.

If you have comments or questions, you can contact me by email at blair@blairhoward.com, and you can visit my website http://www.blairhoward.com.

Thank you. Blair Howard.

If you enjoyed Without Remorse, perhaps you would

like to read the next book in the series, Calaway Jones. You can grab a copy here in the U.S: My Book

Or in the U.K here: My Book

Would you like to read Book 1, Harry Starke, the novel that started it all, for free? If so, just click this link for instant access: http://bit.ly/2hCUa4p

-----

Made in the USA
Las Vegas, NV
23 October 2020